Dr. Frankenstein

By: Mary Reason Theriot

Dedication

Without the love and support of my family and friends I would not have pursued this new path in life. I would especially like to thank those that have proofread copy after copy, to give me their honest opinion of the books.

Yuri and Theresa, thank you so much for your continued encouragement.

To my wonderful husband, Malwen, your continued love and support means the world to me.   I don't know what I would do without you in my life.

A special thank you to Kevin Broussard for encouraging me to write this book. I enjoyed bouncing some of the ideas off of you.

To my fans, I would like to offer a special thank you for your continued support.

Also Available in eBook and Paperback by Mary Reason Theriot

The Hideaway

The Traveler

www.maryreasontheriot.com

ISBN-10: 1-945393-08-4
ISBN-13: 978-1-945393-08-2

Prologue

Judges, lawyers, corporate executives, high school principals, stock brokers, bankers, and people from all walks of life, at some time will cling to their miserable existence. That is where doctors come in. Doctors are the protectors of mankind, the healers and caretakers of our utter existence. Even ancient civilizations revered the medicine man as having special power to safeguard life. The trust of a physician is understood to be sacred. A physician swears to practice medicine ethically and honestly, this is called the Hippocratic Oath.

Granted, most patients know when they will have surgery, but sometimes the tragedies happen. Hospitals and patients depend on a specialized surgeon to heal serious wounds and save patients' lives. These surgeons are known as trauma surgeons. They specialize in performing operations on patients brought into hospital emergency rooms and medical centers. The profession of a trauma surgeon is intense and arduous. The job is extremely high-stress and unpredictable. Trauma surgeons must handle tense situations on a daily basis and handle each case in a professional manner, regardless of whether the patient will survive.

Trauma surgeons operate on the most critical and life-threatening injuries that come through the hospital doors. These patients suffer from acute traumatic and life-threatening diseases and injuries. No matter how trying the case is, the amount of blood being lost, the patient's screams, or the gruesomeness of an injury; the trauma surgeon must not exhibit fear. Nothing can affect the trauma surgeon's ability to critically assess and provide care for even the most severely injured trauma patient.

The trauma surgeon must exhibit competency, strength and confidence. His surgical procedures must be done with exact precision. Trauma surgeons must know how to perform optimally under intense pressure in highly stressful situations. Manual dexterity, attention to detail and excellent communication skills are mandatory qualities of a trauma surgeon. The nurses, trauma team and staff look to the trauma surgeon for supervision, guidance and direction.

During World War II, several German physicians performed excruciating and often deadly experiments on thousands of concentration camp prisoners without their approval. This practice of medicine by these doctors of the Third Reich was egregious, disgraceful, and inexcusable. The Nazi doctors desecrated the trust placed in them by humanity. Worse, most of these doctors escaped their crimes against humanity and went on to live normal lives, unlike their victims.

What would happen if you had a surgeon who likes to play God in his own unique way, similar to that of the Nazi doctors? A surgeon that has a curiosity unlike any other doctor you have encountered?

What would happen if the doctor you entrusted your life with deserted you on the operating table? There have been times when I considered doing that too; walking away while you are at your most vulnerable. At the last moment I swoop in and proceed with the surgery.

Chapter 1

Let me introduce myself. I am Dr. Anthony Habersham, a prestigious trauma surgeon at St. Anne's Hospital in Springport, Louisiana. St. Anne's Hospital is one of the few hospitals in the area with a specialized trauma center. The trauma surgeons and anesthesiologists are available 24/7. This means we are kept busy. Unlike other doctors, trauma surgeons have anonymity. In medical school this was one thing that lured me to trauma surgery. I did not want the same mundane patients and cases day after day. I did not want to be involved in the patient's life. I wanted to keep things clinical. I am not very personable.

Some of my colleagues describe me as detached from my patients, with almost too much clinical precision. Patients and colleagues consider my bedside manner to be atrocious. Over the course of my career, I have cared for thousands of critically wounded and gravely ill patients. I have crossed paths with individuals from every walk of life, from the rich and prestigious to the poor. Regardless of the patient's status in life, they are the same to me – a patient on MY operating table. I have treated gunshot wounds, stabbings, impalement injuries, car accidents, industrial accidents, crush injuries and any other gruesome injury imaginable. I have seen death up close and personal.

I am forty-eight years old and enjoy my single life. I will never make a good husband or father. I rarely sleep at home. I work one hundred twenty-plus hours a week. This is my life, and I like it. Don't try to change me. I sometimes spend my entire day and night in one operating room or another. I basically live at the hospital. I made sure, much to the appreciation of the other surgeons, the on-call room was furnished to my liking. The hospital had no objections as long as they did not have to incur any of the expenses.

I don't care what others think of me. Whether you think my decision is right or wrong, you will listen to what I have to say. Do not question me, ever. Especially in the operating room, that is my domain. I know what I am doing; just do what I tell you.

When I am in the operating room, I remain focused on the task at hand. I may curse and yell at the attendings and nurses, but I am the surgeon! While you are under sedation on my operating table, you are under my control. You are vulnerable, totally dependent on me. I can do whatever I want to your body. I am superb at what I do, and don't you ever doubt it. Those working for me know better than to second guess any decision I make. They will never question me, or else.

When I had you on my operating table last night, I could have killed you. I could have, but I didn't. However, I can't guarantee any other minor changes I may have performed on your body won't kill you later on in life, but for now, you will continue on living your pitiful life. I do not consider myself an angel of mercy. I have a reason behind any modifications I may perform to your body; it is because I can, and there is nothing anyone can do about it. I have an excellent memory and don't forget those who have wronged me. You better pray you never need me as your trauma surgeon. I will not kill you on the operating table, but I will maim or infect you in some way.

I have been told I am a vindictive person, and they are right. It doesn't take much to piss me off.

Today is like any other day at work for me. I slept at the hospital once again, operating into the wee hours of the morning. Somewhere in this city a future patient of mine is also waking up, unaware that they will find themselves in the hospital in the not so distant future. They will find themselves on a gurney being wheeled down the long hallway into the cold, windowless operating room where I will be waiting. Their biggest worry will be of any potential pain afterwards, or maybe if the surgery will leave a scar, but those are petty things to fear. What they should fear is me, and what possible harm I may do to them. Will I, or won't I experiment on this next patient? I won't know until the next opportune moment.

Chapter 2

When Cory Wilson woke up this morning, he had no idea what this day would entail. It started out as a typical day. He rummaged through the small kitchen in the apartment above the garage but didn't find anything appetizing. He knows his mom will have something cooked, so he decides to head over there.

When Cory turned eighteen, he begged his mom and dad to let him move out to the small apartment over the garage. Cory couldn't afford his own place, but he wanted somewhere he could sneak his girlfriends into. Also, he and his friends needed a place where they could hang out without his little brother interfering. His parents reluctantly agreed as long as he kept it clean.

Cory's twenty-first birthday is in a few days, and he still hasn't decided what to do with his life. He tried college, but it wasn't for him. He flunked miserably his first year. He is currently floating from job to job. A career, or work for that matter, isn't important to him. All Cory needs is enough money to go out and party with, and if he doesn't have that, his mom will always give him spending money. Of course she makes him promise he will at least cut the grass, which he never does. His dad keeps telling him to grow up and do something with his life. Cory isn't worried about that. He's still young, and there is plenty of time before he has to worry about money. Besides, his parents pay for his car, insurance, phone, and any other bills he may have. His current lifestyle is perfect. It is low maintenance, and most importantly, stress free. As long as his parents keep paying his way in life, he plans on keeping it this way.

Cory is currently working in construction. The money is good and the hours aren't bad. He is home before nightfall and can go party. The energy drinks help him get going in the morning after a late night.

***

Trish Wilson hears Cory walking down the inside stairs to the house. She laughs to herself. He must need breakfast as usual.

Cory gives his mom a quick hug. "Morning mom."

She fixes him a plate of scrambled eggs and bacon. "Did you want a piece of toast?"

"I'm good. This is perfect. Thanks."

Trish looks over at her son. Cory looks more like his dad every day. He is a handsome young man, standing over six feet tall. He has his father's sharp features, piercing blue eyes and dark wavy hair. If only he had his father's work ethic.

She won't tell him to his face, to avoid any possible conflict, but she secretly wishes he would grow up. He has no ambition in life. It is frustrating to see him living his life this way. She assumed he would make something of himself. Unless he has to work, he will sleep the day away. He would sleep his life away if he could. Maybe she is to blame though, she has over-indulged him. Perhaps she should listen to her husband, Jim. He suggested they charge Cory rent. At the very least, they make him pay his car insurance and phone bill. If he refuses, all she has to do is cancel the insurance and phone. That will get her son's attention. He views his phone not as a luxury, but as his lifeline. He would be lost without it. The car would have to sit in the driveway until he gets off his ass to earn enough money to pay the bill.

Trish doesn't understand kids these days. Even his friends seem to have no ambition in life. By the time she was Cory's age, she was finishing college and planning her upcoming wedding. What is this world coming to? These kids are entering adulthood with a high school education, no real job, no money and worst of all, no plans in life.

"Thanks for the breakfast mom. I'm off to work."

"Be careful. See you tonight."

***

Jim and Trish Wilson are sitting in the ER waiting room, anxiously awaiting news on their son, Cory. He was involved in a serious accident at work. For an unknown reason, a crane dropped its cargo too early and Cory was injured.

I receive the call for an emergency surgery right before lunch. A young man has received multiple facial lacerations, a broken nose that needs to be reset and a crushed hand. CT scans have been completed, and no other injuries are noted. I find myself wondering what I would do if I were in his position. My hands are my most valuable asset, without them I could not perform surgery. I actually have an insurance policy on my hands, just in case something ever happens to them. My hands are my livelihood.

The human hand is comprised of numerous little bones, all working together to help complete its function. What will happen if one of these small bones is inadvertently left out during surgery? Will the hand still function in the same manner? This might be the perfect time for an experiment.

The hospital's top trauma nurse, Carol Boudreaux, notifies me that no one has informed the parents as to the extent of their son's injuries. Nurse Boudreaux is a wonderful, caring nurse and I delegate this task to her. She makes up for my foul bedside manner.

If I were looking to have a quick fling, Nurse Boudreaux is the type of woman I would go for. She is exceptionally attractive. Unlike many other nurses here, she keeps herself in shape. She is quite tall for a woman, maybe around five feet ten inches with delicate facial bones. She has long, wavy auburn hair and eyes that remind me of a rich coffee. Some men would deem her a classic beauty. Since most of the time her face is spent behind a surgical mask, she always makes sure her eyes are well defined with makeup, alluding to the beauty underneath the mask. In my opinion, she looks better without makeup.

An hour after Cory Wilson is rushed to the emergency room, he is whisked off to the operating room. Nurse Boudreaux and the rest of the OR team are busy setting up their stations, unfolding sterile blue drapes, making sure the lights are set correctly, and arranging the sterilized instruments. There isn't much conversation taking place in the room, everyone is too busy working.

A nurse is busy prepping Mr. Wilson for his surgery. I don my mask and scrub in. Once I am through scrubbing my hands and arms, a nurse helps dress me in a gown and gloves, so as to not contaminate myself. Mr. Wilson is secured to the gurney to prevent him from falling off before or after anesthesia is administered. Nurses are busy counting sponges and instruments; this is to ensure that everything is accounted for once the surgery is complete. Now if a surgeon were to slip his own sponges into the operating room, the nursing staff would never know if a sponge was left in the patient, but that will not happen for this surgery.

When I enter the room there is a flurry of activity still taking place, a lab tech is drawing more blood, and the x-ray tech is setting up the films of the patient's hand and his head. When I was an intern, I learned how to read x-ray films. I never trust anyone to read the patient's films for me. Some radiologists tend to miss serious injuries.

The anesthesiologist is busy preparing the medications and equipment he will be using. The patient's blood pressure and breathing will be monitored closely while he is under anesthesia.

The room is silent except for the nurse counting backwards with the patient. Most of the items in the room are covered in green to signify their sterilization. Once the anesthesia has been administered, the patient will also be draped in green. Mr. Wilson's hand has been placed on a separate table in order for me to operate on it. His face will be covered with a sterilized green sheet, minus a hole for his face. I plan on resetting the nose as soon as I complete the operation on the hand. The intravenous IV, drip has been started on Mr. Wilson's uninjured arm, to not impede the operation. Due to the patient's broken nose, he has to breathe through his mouth. I tap my foot, hoping the staff will soon realize that I am growing impatient and ready to begin.

The young man and his parents are thrilled that the surgery was successful. By all accounts, my surgeries are always flawless, except for some minor modifications I may have secretly performed.

If problems associated with my experiments are discovered after the surgery, I prefer to leave the blame and headaches involved, on the hospital. Let them do the worrying. I try to limit myself to performing experimental procedures that will be difficult to prove the injury occurred while I was the surgeon. Hopefully, by the time any malpractice is noticed, the focus will be away from me, far away. So far I have been fortunate, and this has been the case. Sometimes it is years before any problems arise from my experiments, or not at all.

This may be the case with this young man. There is no telling how long before I will know about any complications associated with my modifications to his hand, if any problems even develop.

Call it sadistic if you must, but curiosity gets the best of me and I want to see what will happen if something is taken from or introduced into a patient. Lately, I have become curious about different medical scenarios. I keep journals recording every experiment I have performed and the results. A medical malpractice attorney would love to get his hands on my journals, if they ever knew they existed.

If you need to be operated on, truth be told, you want me in that room. I should make myself clear, you should want me to operate, but not perform any of my little experiments on you. These experiments, though, are what get me through all the tedious surgeries. However, I'm not a complete monster. Not all of my patients will have experiments performed on them, only a select few.

There have been times during my career that I went days without performing an operation. Then there are days that I never know a new day has begun because an emergency surgery needed to be performed in the middle of the night. On slow days, I have nothing to do besides plot and plan.

I am an adrenaline junkie. I have a need to play God on a daily basis. When there is a lull in emergencies, I go crazy. How difficult would it be to cause a car accident with severe injuries? Or maybe I could walk into a department store and start shooting people? Anything to bring me more patients to operate on! But the Hippocratic Oath keeps me from intentionally bringing harm to any patient, or does it?

Chapter 3

Dale Hebert knows he is too drunk to drive home, but it's a long walk from the bar to his house. If he keeps his speed to a crawl, he will be fine. He's been drunker than this and driven home with no problems. He never sees the tree when he veers off the road. He hears the sound of crunching metal and glass shattering, but it seems so far-off. He watches as his world slowly disintegrates into darkness. Thankfully a passerby notices the accident and calls the paramedics.

Dale keeps wondering where the flashing lights are coming from. A red light keeps flashing in the dark recesses of his mind. He keeps hearing someone groaning, too, after a few minutes he realizes it is him. His head is killing him. He must have one hell of a hangover. Besides the remnants of beer, he tastes something else in his mouth. It's not something he is familiar with though, maybe blood? He must have split his lip open last night and not realized it. How much did he have to drink at the bar?

Dale keeps hearing someone talking to him, but it is so hard to concentrate on the voice with so many other noises, "Sir, what's your name? I need you to keep still. We will have you out as soon as we can."

Dale's vision finally comes into focus. He isn't at home. Where the hell is he? He hears the man talking again, "Sir, you have several superficial lacerations to your face and upper body, but your legs are pinned. We are working on freeing you as fast as we can. Do you understand?''

Dale nods his head. In a shaky voice he asks, "What happened? Where am I?"

"You were in an accident, sir. Can you please tell me your name?"

"Dale."

"Dale, my name is Josh. You will be all right, but I need you to stay calm. The fire department will have you out of your truck in a few more minutes."

Dale tries to move and feels a searing pain move down his legs. "Sir, please, you have to stay still. It is important that you stay still. Just try to relax."

Dale nods his head once again. He is getting agitated. Why can't they get him out of here? He hears the sirens from the fire truck and ambulance; they are making his headache even worse than it already is. As they free him from the wreckage, the pain flares up even more from the sudden movement. He feels the weight of the truck lift off his lower body.

It has taken the firemen and paramedics a while to extract him from the vehicle. They ended up having to use the Jaws of Life. Dale is just glad to be free.

* * *

I receive the call for an emergency surgery around two a.m. A man has received multiple facial and upper body lacerations along with two crushed legs. The orthopedic surgeon is tied up, and tonight's on-call trauma surgeon is currently operating on another patient. The emergency room doctor wants to know if I can perform the surgery. I inform him I will be there shortly; go ahead and prep the patient.

I drive my Aston Martin DB9 coupe to the hospital. This car may be my one true love in life. There is an overwhelming feeling of power when I drive it. The vehicle that I drive must match my personality. This one does that beyond my expectations; it is almost as if we are connected spiritually. The raw power that I experience while driving it is truly incredible. No other car can match its style, beauty and speed. With the roads devoid of traffic, and the speed of the car, I reach my destination in no time.

This surgery will be the perfect time to implement my latest trial. Everyone knows hospitals are breeding grounds for staph infections. Hospitals are also known for a specific staph infection, Methicillin Resistant Staphylococcus Aureus – also known as MRSA.   It can be transmitted in numerous ways, such as a lazy housekeeper deciding to use the same contaminated cloth to clean the whole floor she is assigned to. It can even be spread by a nurse or doctor failing to wash his or her hands properly while moving from room to room checking on patients. Or worse, it could be caused by a surgeon deliberately introducing it into the body to see how long it goes unnoticed by the nurses. It will be quite easy, while I am repairing this patient's wound, I will introduce the bacteria into his surgical site. No one will notice, and if they do notice anything out of the ordinary, they know better than to question my motives. No one dares to confront me regarding medical issues, fearing being ridiculed in front of their colleagues. It may take a while before a nurse notices that this poor man has contracted a staph infection. Only time will tell if they catch it soon enough. Will this patient end up losing one or both of his legs, or maybe even his life, before the staph infection is discovered and treated?

After the surgery the family will want answers. The patient will want to know if he will ever walk again. I won't have the heart to tell them that his time on this planet may be short lived. I hate giving people false hope, his survival and recovery will depend on how fast someone notices the infection. The patient's life is of no concern to me, I will have completed my little experiment and wait to see the outcome.

But, of course, my surgery will be impeccable as always. I have never lost a patient on the operating table at this or any other hospital I have worked at. Now, if or when the patient dies after the surgery is of no consequence to me.

As I enter the hospital, I inhale deeply. While most smell the distinct antiseptic aroma, I smell power. I am getting ready to change the life of one man. Every day patients come into this hospital in need of a doctor. A patient will look to me to save their miserable life. I am a vital part to their survival; or am I?

I walk down the long hallway to the operating room, and I notice all the activity going on in the hospital tonight. Normally at this time of the night this area is devoid of the cacophony of sounds that resonate through the hospital during the day, but tonight it is bustling with activity.

The OR team is busy setting up their stations, unfolding sterile green drapes, making sure the lights are set correctly and spreading out the sterilized instruments. As I enter the room there is a flurry of activity. The x-ray tech is setting up the films of the patient's injuries. An extensive amount of damage seems to have been done to the patient's legs.

A few minutes later, I am scrubbed and ready to begin the operation, "Alright, let's get ready to operate."

We have already been operating on the patient for a while when the anesthesiologist states, "Blood pressure dropped. How's it going?"

"I'm finishing up the hardware right now. How bad is it?"

I get impatient when I have to stop an operation; especially one of this magnitude.

"Just dropped a fraction. I will give him a unit of blood."

I see the circulating nurse hang a unit of blood from the IV pole. Suddenly the room is quiet. All you hear is the hissing rasp of the ventilator and the steady beeping of the heart monitor. "Pressure is coming back up."

This patient will have enough hardware in his legs to open his own hardware store by the time this is done. I give a fixator nut one last meticulous turn.

Before moving on, I ask the anesthesiologist, "How is he doing?"

"Okay for now. How much longer do you think?"

"At least another hour or so. Both legs are shattered. They need to be pinned, and he will be in traction for a while."

The surgery ends up taking a little over twelve hours to complete, and all goes according to plan.

Chapter 4

When Dale wakes up in the hospital, he notices his wife sitting in the chair next to the bed. She must have seen his eyes fluttering because she moves closer to the bed and holds his hand. "You gave me quite a scare. Are you okay?"

"Legs hurt."

"Your legs are in traction for now. The doctor will be here soon to explain what was done during surgery."

"What happened?"

"You were in an accident. Do you remember anything at all?"

"No, I don't. Oh God, did I hurt anyone else? Please tell me I didn't kill anyone?"

"It was a one car accident, but you were drunk."

Dale is so ashamed. He knows better than to drink and drive. He honestly didn't think he had all that much to drink. "What about the truck?"

"It's totaled. You wrapped it around a tree. Geez, Dale, you are extremely lucky you didn't die in the accident."

The conversation is too exhausting, and before Dale can talk to the doctor about the burning pain in his leg, he falls back asleep. Nurses come in out and of his room, checking his vital signs and giving medicines. Every time Dale wakes up, his wife is right there at his side, either napping or reading a book. Dale takes some comfort that she hasn't left his side during this whole ordeal. How could he have been so stupid, drinking and driving? He knew better!

The pain in Dale Hebert's leg is excruciating. He has complained to the orthopedic surgeon several times now, but to no avail. The doctor merely treats him like a drunk that can't get alcohol and is trying to get drugs instead. That is not the case. Dale may go to the bar occasionally and get drunk, but he is not an alcoholic by any means. He is in severe pain, though, and wishes someone would take him seriously.

"I'm telling you Dr. Cole, one leg is throbbing more than the other one, something isn't right. It feels as if it is on fire."

***

Dr. Jeffery Cole has been an orthopedic surgeon for five years now. His latest patient has been a problem patient from the beginning. Dr. Cole prefers to be the one to operate on his orthopedic patients, but he was tied up when Mr. Hebert's accident happened. He has reviewed Dr. Habersham's notes, and by all accounts, Dr. Habersham did a bang up job.

"Mr. Hebert, I can write an order for an x-ray, and make sure the leg is set correctly if that will help put your mind at ease."

"Anything, please! The pain is awful."

"You have to understand that you have several pins and screws in your legs due to the accident. Both your legs have been rebuilt and the healing process will be painful for quite a while."

Dr. Cole writes the orders for the x-ray, just to put Mr. Hebert's mind at ease. He doesn't expect to find anything except a leg healing.

The overhead page has Dr. Cole rushing to x-ray. The technician is waiting for him. "Dr. Cole, the radiologist asked that you come up here immediately. It looks like MRSA has developed in the man's leg."

Dr. Cole knows this isn't good at all. MRSA is a bacterium that causes infections in different parts of the body. It's much tougher to treat than most strains of staph because it is resistant to most of the common antibiotics. MRSA can infect surgical wounds, the bloodstream, the lungs, or the urinary tract.

Mr. Hebert's cast is removed and treatment is started on the infected leg. Hopefully they can contain this "super bug" before it spreads any further. Maybe they can save the leg from amputation. Without the cast, his leg will have to be immobilized. "Mr. Hebert, it looks like your stay in our lovely little facility will be extended for a while longer."

As each day passes, Mr. Hebert looks worse. He now looks like a critically ill patient. The MRSA is spreading faster than they can control it. The leg has to be amputated. Dr. Cole hates breaking the news to the patient. As he enters the private room, Dr. Cole notices his patients' eyes are dull and listless; the eyes of death. You can see the utter defeat in Mr. Hebert's attitude.

Dale Hebert's health is clearly on a steep downward spiral. Though most MRSA infections aren't usually life-threatening, they sometimes can be. Unfortunately, it looks as if Mr. Hebert's body is rapidly losing its battle against MRSA. Dr. Cole hates this part of his job. Being in orthopedics, he has rarely had to inform a patient or their loved ones of an impending death. In his field, it doesn't occur that often.

***

The room is wrapped in the silence that inevitably follows a patient's death as the nurses and various health care workers slowly leave the room. An intern is asked to stay behind and prepare the body, so the deceased's loved ones can see him one last time before he is moved to the morgue.

Dr. Cole sits down next to the deceased's wife. "Mrs. Hebert, I am so sorry. Dale put up a good fight, but due to his injuries, his body could not fight off the infection. Even after amputating his leg it spread into his blood stream. We tried everything possible to save him."

Sobs shake her little body, "I don't understand how this could happen. He had two broken legs, how did he contract staph?"

"Unfortunately, sometimes it happens in hospitals."

"Oh God, what am I going to do now? Dale was the one who brought home the money while I stayed home with our two kids. He is the one who had our health insurance."

Dr. Cole isn't sure what else to say. He can only try to comfort the poor, grieving woman

"Would you like some time alone with your husband?"

"Yes. Thank you."

"Is there anyone I can call to come be with you?"

"My mother is watching the kids for me."

"Why don't you give me her number and I'll ask her to come, then she can take you home."

"Thank you."

"Mrs. Hebert, again, I am so very sorry. I tried everything in my power to save your husband."

"I just don't understand it. He wasn't even a heavy drinker. This could have all been prevented. Why did he have to get behind that wheel drunk?"

Dr. Cole doesn't say anything. Nothing he can say will help her feel better or to understand why this happened. He has seen too many lives affected by drinking and driving. Dr. Cole goes back to his office to make the call and to dictate his report. There will be a peer review to see what went wrong. He wishes he knew how this happened. The hospital will also come under scrutiny for another MRSA death. He doesn't understand it. MRSA seemed to be under control in the hospital. Very few outbreaks have occurred in quite a while.

***

Kirstin Hebert enters the room where her husband's body is. She grasps his cold hand while the tears spill from her eyes, "Oh Dale, I know you didn't mean to leave me like this. At least you are at peace now. Please don't worry about us, we will always love you. I will make sure the kids never forget you. It may take a while for things to fall back into place, but we will survive."

By now the tears are flowing down Kirstin's face. She leans down and kisses Dale one last time. It is still impossible to fathom that she will never feel his lips kissing her, never again be held in his tight embrace and made love to.

Chapter 5

Kirstin Hebert cannot believe she is planning her husband's funeral. Everything seems to happen so fast. Both children are inconsolable with grief. Thankfully, her mother is watching them today so that she can get this part behind her. Dale had been such a good husband and father. He had been her best friend. She doesn't know how she will survive without him.

She is meeting with the funeral director of Darden and Sons Funeral Home. He is a nice young man, who has promised to help guide her through this difficult process.

With tears glimmering in her eyes, "Mr. Darden, thank you for taking the time to help me. My husband and I never really talked about our deaths, but he had mentioned that he would like to be cremated and have his ashes spread across the bayou. He complained about how he never had time to visit his parents' gravesite. I think it bothered him that he never made it over there."

"Cremation is not a problem. Did you want to pick out an urn?"

"No, I'll let you handle that. Just pick out something simple, please. His life insurance should be enough to cover the funeral expenses."

It doesn't take long for the arrangements to be made. Kirstin wants a small wake the night before he is to be cremated so that the children can say goodbye to their father one last time.

When Kirstin makes it back to her parents' house, she notices her brother is also there. Bill never really liked Dale, so she's not sure if she is up to handling his company today.

"Sis, I am so sorry."

"Thanks Bill."

"Do you have a moment to talk? I'm worried about you and the kids."

"Let's go into the kitchen. I could use a cup of coffee."

"I'm not trying to interfere in your life, but how are you set up financially?"

"It's not good. Some months we barely make it. His 401K doesn't have that much in it after the recession. His life insurance policy is going to be enough to cremate him. Mom will watch the kids so I can go back to work. That's not how either of us wanted to raise the kids, but I don't have a choice. I'm hoping the insurance company will at least pay off the loan on Dale's truck so I don't have to worry about the note. My car was paid off a few months ago. I have no idea what his medical bills will be. I'm sure they will be astronomical though. He was in ICU after the MRSA spread, plus he had the two leg surgeries."

"I need you to really listen to what I have to say. You need to meet with a medical malpractice attorney, now, not later. The hospital is responsible for Dale's death. They should pay for his funeral and drop all medical bills. Plus, they should offer you a cash settlement."

"I don't know Bill. I've never even thought of suing someone in the past. I have always thought of lawsuits as frivolous."

"Kirstin, the hospital is responsible. It is because of the MRSA that Dale is dead. You need to talk to a lawyer, if not for you, then for the kids. They may offer you a big enough settlement where you can at least make ends meet now that Dale is gone."

"How do I even find an attorney?"

"Let me make some calls for you."

"Thanks. This is just all too much for me to take in right now."

It has been three weeks since her husband's funeral and Kirstin Hebert is still trying to cope with everything. The first weeks following his death have been worse than she expected. Thankfully, she has her family and friends to offer their support.

It is time to pull her life together. She will miss her husband dearly, but her kids need her. She needs to get on with her life. Lying in bed, depressed won't help her or the kids. With Dale gone she has a lot of responsibilities that lay on her shoulders now.

Chapter 6

The Stanfords are a nice young couple. Their six year old daughter, Jessica, was in an unfortunate accident. While jumping on her brand new trampoline, practicing her flips, she fell off and broke her ankle, or shattered it to be more specific. Little Jessica has a bad break and will need a few pins to help the break heal right. The on-call orthopedic surgeon is busy with another operation, and due to budget cuts there is no other orthopedic surgeon currently on staff. This is where I come in.

Larry Stevens has been the hospital administrator for the past fifteen years. He knows personality clashes, power plays and political machinations are omnipresent and as integral a part of the hospital as IV's and bedpans. With that being said, he has a hard time getting along with the more difficult surgeons here. Their super-sized egos are more than he can take most days. Larry Stevens also understands that without managed care and effective peer review in the hospital, the doctors here would do as they pleased.

When I was hired, Larry informed me he didn't like me or my attitude. He feels that I am an arrogant bastard. I feel the same way about him. We also agree to disagree about certain hospital policies.

"Dr. Habersham, wait up a minute please." states Larry Stevens.

I groan. I don't need this right now.

"Dr. Habersham, it is imperative that you meet with the Stanfords before you operate."

I inform him in no uncertain terms, "Larry, I have no intentions of meeting with the Stanfords before their daughter's surgery." It is hilarious watching him turn beet red.

"Why must you be so insufferable? These parents are worried sick about their child. Have you no compassion in you to put their minds at ease before you operate on their daughter. The mother is beside herself with worry."

"Well, she should be. What kind of irresponsible parent does not at least put up the netting included with the trampoline? This could have been prevented."

"Don't you dare make these parents feel worse than they do already! Honestly, I don't understand why we seem to have this conversation before every surgery. People need reassurance that everything will be okay. They want to have faith in the doctor that is getting ready to perform the operation. If you had a caring bone in your body, you would understand. I wish the Board had never hired you, but that was not my decision. They knew about your atrocious bedside manner and hired you anyway. You make my job unbearable at times."

Richard Stanford is a prominent citizen in Springport, even though he is only in his early thirty's. He is a successful businessman and investor, having several business interests around town, including a hotel and an apartment complex. It is rumored he has invested in a strip mall and a few restaurants around town. Mr. Stanford has a high energy level and a very astute business sense that have both helped him have such a financial success at an early age. Richard Stanford sees opening businesses as a game. He has a fierce competitive streak. He is also a very devoted husband and father.

Mr. and Mrs. Stanford are both from Springport, Louisiana and have many prominent ties to the community. Their prominence in the community does not bother me, but I can tell it worries Larry Stevens. "Their influence means nothing to me. I will set her ankle and that is it. If you think their asses need kissing so bad, then go handle that yourself. Do you really want me talking to them?"

I don't have the heart to tell Larry the real reason I prefer not to meet the Stanfords. Jessica's unfortunate accident has me wondering. What would happen if I inadvertently remove a small portion of her ankle bone? Will it heal correctly? Will she be able to walk properly? We will have to wait and watch little Jessica grow to answer these questions. Very few pediatric cases come through the doors as traumas, and this may be my only chance for a while. There is no possible way I can look them in their eyes and tell them everything will be okay considering what I have planned.

"I've got to run. The OR is calling for me." I can tell that he is unhappy with me for brushing him off. As I head to the elevators to leave there is a group of people waiting. I don't want to give Larry another chance to start up this conversation again so instead of waiting I took the stairs two at a time.

Little Jessica Stanford is terrified. The nurse tells her that the doctor is getting ready to fix her ankle so it won't hurt as bad anymore. She will be as good as new in several weeks. "Jessica honey, what color cast would you like the doctor to put on you once he has fixed your ankle?"

Jessica thinks about the question, as if it is the most important thing she has been asked all day, "Do you have yellow?"

"We sure do."

"I want…… pink."

The nurse chuckles, "Pink then, not yellow?"

"Yep, pink."

***

Jessica wants her mom to be in the room with her. She could walk with her to this big room, but she isn't allowed inside. Now all she can do is lie on this hard bed and look at the bright lights overhead.

The nurse is explaining that they will put a mask on her face and she will need to count to ten. "Jessica honey, do you know how to count to ten?"

Jessica thinks that is a funny question to ask. After all, she is six years old now, and in the first grade, she is a big girl. "Yes, ma'am. Why can't my mommy stay with me?"

"Your mommy is right outside the door waiting for you to get better. It will be all right. Would you like a pair of earphones and listen to some music while you count to ten? It might help you relax?"

"Uh-uh. I want my mommy." Even though the nurse is pretty and very nice, Jessica still wants her mommy. This place scares her and it is cold. Jessica decides maybe since they aren't letting her have her mommy, she should try the music. Asking for her over and over isn't working with this lady like it does with her mommy. She is scared to put on the mask. Pouting, she tells the nurse, "I can try the music now."

***

Nurse Boudreaux is thankful the young girl has decided to listen to some music. Maybe the anesthesiologist can have her put under before Dr. Habersham arrives. He doesn't take kindly to whining children. He would probably make the child even more nervous. If the little girl gets upset and cries it will take even longer to put her under. Handing Jessica the earphones she explains, "Okay Jessica, let's put these on. While you are listening to the music can you count to ten for me? I bet you are asleep before you can finish."

"Uh-huh, I'm smart. I know how to count. Counting to ten is really easy for me."

"Well, let's see how fast you can count then."

"One… Two… Three… Four… Five… Six… Seve……."

Little Jessica Stanford is sound asleep moments before I walk into the operating room. The risks and challenges of

this surgery excite me. I am elated with anticipation. If only
I could look into the future and see what will happen.

***

Richard and Eve Stanford patiently wait for any news
regarding their daughter's operation. Richard has always
been the one in control, and this time he has no control of
the outcome. This is something he is not comfortable with
at all.

Chapter 7

Shane Bryant has to run to the gas station down the road
from where he lives to get his mom a gallon of milk. Before
he got his license he couldn't wait to drive. He didn't expect
his mom to jump on the bandwagon so quickly and have
him running errands. He wouldn't doubt she forgot the milk
when she was shopping, just to make him get off the
computer and out of the house. She has something against
him relaxing. She constantly nags him about playing video
games.

There is no way he is going all the way to the grocery store
when he can dash into the gas station. Plus they are
cheaper on milk and he can pocket the change. His mom
doesn't like him stopping off at this gas station. It seems to
have a lot of robberies, even during the day. She worries
too much. Nothing happens in broad daylight.

Shane never sees the gunman running from the store, he is
too busy texting his girlfriend. He does feel the bullet as it
rips through his flesh though. The pain is too excruciating
to answer the paramedics as they ask him questions. He
begs them to call his mom.

***

A fresh trail of blood leads from the ambulance docking
area to the trauma room. The medics rush the patient into
the hospital. The red glare of the lights dances off the
freshly waxed floor of the emergency room. The teenager is
losing blood fast, and they need to get him stabilized. The
young patient is surrounded by a swarm of nurses,

orderlies, lab and x-ray techs, busily prepping their newest patient for surgery.

Nurse Boudreaux wants to get as much accomplished as she can before calling Dr. Habersham. There is no sense in getting him riled up before surgery. He prefers as little contact with the patient as possible; his main concern is the surgery. With Dr. Habersham's atrocious bedside manner, it is best that this patient not talk to the doctor before surgery, no sense in upsetting him before the operation. The poor boy has been through enough. She can tell in his eyes that he is terrified.

The x-ray technician is busy taking as many films as possible of the shoulder wound. He will rush the films back to Dr. Habersham stat, so he can get a good look at the injuries before surgery.

Everyone hears the technician yell, "X-ray!" and they dash behind the lead screen set up in the room. Since he is busy rushing through the x-rays it is making it difficult for the nurses to complete their tasks at hand. IV lines have to be inserted and secured into the young man, and blood drawn for labs. The lab tech also needs to cross match his blood type. The poor thing has lost a lot of blood from the gunshot wound and they need to be prepared just in case a transfusion is needed during surgery.

Nurse Jenkins is busy cutting the boy's clothes off. It's such a shame, she thought to herself. This young man was in the wrong place at the wrong time. He was gunned down during broad daylight of all things. What is happening with this world? He looks so young and innocent.

****

The call for the gunshot victim comes in as I am leaving for supper. By the time I have donned my surgical attire, the young patient has already been anesthetized. The patient is prepped and ready. There is no time for a pre-op evaluation. No time to notify the next-of-kin about the upcoming surgery or the injuries he has sustained. That will be left to the police. The bandages on his injured right shoulder are soaked in blood. The artery needs to be quickly repaired in order to stop the bleeding before the shoulder can be put back together. This young man is lucky, if the shooter had better aim he wouldn't be here. It won't take long to repair the damage done by the bullet, but it will be a painful recovery. The wound is a through and through, but the bullet still did a good bit of damage. Several of the bones have been shattered in the shoulder.

The anesthesiologist is complaining about how he didn't have time to question the young man. He had to do an emergency intubation. The anesthesiologist is in a chatty mood, one that I don't want to reciprocate.

Nurse Boudreaux hands me the scalpel and I glance down at the blade in my gloved hands, eyeing the beauty of the surgical steel. The razor sharp edge has a lethal look to it, which in the wrong hands it could be. This one singular instrument gives me total power in this room, the power to harm or heal. I wonder which one it will be today, or will it possibly be both? With me as your surgeon you never know.

Cutting through the skin, I watch as a trail of crimson blood flows from the incision. The reddish blue muscle fibers twitch and spasm as the scalpel rakes across them. One of the scrub nurses wipes my forehead with a sponge. For some reason it is hotter in here than normal, "Can we turn down the temperature a notch or two? Let's try and get this place comfortable."

The OR is wrapped in silence, the ventilator making the only noise.

The surgery takes five hours and goes smoothly. His vital signs remain stable during the entire procedure. The only kink in the surgery is the small one I caused. I couldn't help myself; I left out one of the bone shards that the bullet splintered.

***

Lori Bryant watches as her son lay motionless on the hospital bed. The nurse said the surgery was successful, the gunshot was a through and through. Other than the damage to his shoulder there were no other injuries. Lori's guilt is eating at her. Why did she have to forget the milk when she went grocery shopping? If she hadn't, then Shane wouldn't have had to run out to the store and he wouldn't have been shot. This is all her fault.

She listens to the beeps the monitors are making; somehow the steady, rhythmic sounds are calming her. The beeps indicate her son is alive. Ever since Shane was brought out of surgery, she has not left his side. She has not let go of his hand, refusing to budge. She wants to be here when he wakes, to let him know how sorry she is for making him run to the store. When she looks at her son lying in bed, she doesn't see a teenager, but the scared little five year old who didn't want to leave her side to go to kindergarten. Oh, how she misses those days, time flies by too fast.

She hears the nurse enter the room, "Mrs. Bryant, are you sure I can't get you something to eat or drink? He will be asleep for a little while longer."

"No, I'm good, thank you. I just want to sit here and watch him sleep."

"Yes, ma'am. Please let me know if there is anything at all that you need."

"I will."

At that same moment her cell phone rings. It is Greg. He works offshore, and she has had a hard time reaching him. "Honey, can you hear me? The connection is bad. I just got your message. They are sending the helicopter out to the rig and it should be here shortly. Is he okay?"

"He is out of surgery. The bullet went completely through his shoulder. Thankfully, the only damage done is to his shoulder. The doctor said that it will be a while before he can use his arm again, but thank God he is alive."

"I don't understand why he went to that store. We have told him time and again not to go to that area of town."

"It's entirely my fault. I asked him to pick up some milk, and I guess since it was daylight he figured it would be okay."

"Did they at least catch the guy who shot him?"

"They did. He is in police custody. I don't know too many details. The cops told me they will stop by in the morning to get Shane's statement."

"Is your mom with the kids?"

"She is. Dad will take them to their house tonight. Your parents are on their way to our house. They want to be nearby in case we need anything. I told them they could stay in our room."

"That's fine. I should be home sometime today. I plan on coming directly to the hospital."

Lori can hear the rain hitting against the window. The thunderstorm they had predicted for earlier today must finally be here. The tears that had been threatening to flow break free. The pain and exhaustion of the day win out. Not moving, she lays her head down on the bed next to Shane. She wishes she could wrap her arms around him and hold him as she did when he was little and take all the hurt away. If only this was a nightmare she could wake up from, but it isn't.

Later on that night when Greg walks in the door the tears break free once more. She runs into his arms, feeling some comfort from his embrace. The sobs rack through her body as the stress from the day finds its release.

Chapter 8

Ty Baptiste and Logan Blanchard are revved up from tonight's win. The football game was a close one. The other team was almost as good as them, almost.

Ty is too pumped up to go home. "Dude, let's grab the girls and go to Faux Pas." Faux Pas is a popular night club in Springport where a lot of the locals hang out.

"I don't know man. What if we get busted?"

"Who's going to check out the ID's that closely. I swear they look real. Come on, I know the girls will be up for it."

"I'll go if you can talk Jen into it."

***

Jen Dixon and Amy Wells can't wait to find the guys. Jen hopes the guys are as super psyched about the game as they are.

Jen sees Ty walking over their way and runs up to him, jumping into his arms. "Great game, babe. You played so well tonight. Totally awesome."

Ty gives her a kiss and asks, "Are you all up to going over to Faux Pas and hanging out?"

"I'm game. What about you Amy?"

"My parents think I'm spending the night at your house, so I'm cool with it."

***

Ty can't wait to dance with Jen. "Come on, Logan, let's go man."

Ty and Logan stop off at a local gas station to try out their fake ID's first. They buy a six pack of Bud Light's, without any problem. By the time they reach Faux Pas, they have finished the beer, and are ready to have some fun. The night is still young and both of the girls want to dance.

The parking lot is packed by the time they arrive. They pull into a spot next to a brand new Camaro. Ty looks at it, and knows he could blow that thing away in his Ford Mustang. His convertible looks way cooler anyway. Man, what he wouldn't give to drag race with that car.

When they finally manage to get inside Faux Pas, it is packed. The DJ is playing the music extremely loud while the crowd is dancing, drinking and bumping into each other. There is nowhere to sit, and it is next to impossible to squeeze up to the bar to get a drink. When Ty finally catches the bartender's attention, he orders four beers and they head off to the dance floor to try and find a place to dance.

For the next three hours they drink and dance. By two a.m. the girls are ready to leave. Jen whines, "Come on Ty, I'm hungry. Let's go get something to eat and find a place to park."

Now Ty likes that idea. When they leave the bar, Ty notices the driver of the Camaro getting into it, "Hey Dude, wanna race? I can smoke that car of yours any day!"

"In your dreams! Man, I'll make you run crying back home to your mommy when I wipe the road with you and your car. Let's go."

Jen whines again, "Come on Ty, that's not what we are supposed to be doing."

"Come on Jen. This won't take long and then I'll go get you a pizza or something. Let me do this baby."

She huffs, but caves in, "Oh, fine! Just hurry up."

Jen slides into the front with Ty, and Logan and Amy get in the back seat. Both cars pull out of the parking lot and meet up at a traffic light. Ty rolls down Jen's window to talk to the other driver. "As soon as the next light turns green we go. First one to the next light wins."

"I'm ready man, let's do this."

Ty isn't worried about the cops. It's too early in the morning, and besides there is no one around. As they near the intersection, the mustang is pushing seventy. The Camaro is right beside him. Ty is busy paying attention to the Camaro that he doesn't notice the light ahead turning red and another car, a black BMW, pulling out to turn. The collision is violent. The impact creates an ear piercing sound of crashing metal and exploding glass. The brief, panic-stricken screams echo in the night. The immense force has reduced the vehicles involved into twisted metal, almost unrecognizable. The Camaro has somehow avoided being added to the mound of twisted metal; it flipped over several times and finally landed upside down.   The Mustang and BMW are inseparable. Neither Logan nor Amy was wearing seat belts, and they are ejected from the car on impact. Jen is turned towards Ty, but she is wearing her seat belt. Her lower body is trapped between what's left of the seat and dash. Even though Ty is not wearing his seatbelt, the air bag somehow stopped him from flying through the windshield, but he has suffered a large laceration across his forehead and his face is severely injured. He is pinned between the steering wheel and the front seat of his car. He can barely breathe, and he can't move his legs. Within minutes the sound of sirens fills the night air.

***

Nurse Jenkins takes the call from the ambulance. "Just wanted to give you a heads up, we are headed your way with four trauma cases. Motor vehicle accident involving three vehicles; ETA is five minutes. Two teenagers are in bad shape, and you can smell the alcohol on them, so you will need to run the appropriate blood work. The driver of one vehicle tried avoiding the accident, but he still got injured pretty bad, and the driver of the car that they hit is barely hanging on."

Nurse Jenkins hates motor vehicle accidents. The carnage they can leave behind is worse than you can ever imagine. "I'll let the trauma surgeons know."

Nurse Jenkins calls Dr. Habersham, since he is at the hospital, "Dr. Habersham, we have trauma times five arriving in four minutes. Medics say they are barely holding on."

***

I was unable to sleep and had stepped outside to enjoy a cigar and the night air. The silvery light of the moon gives the night a calming effect. Even the stars are out tonight. It is hospital policy that the on call physician must not leave the vicinity, but I see no harm in stepping outside to smoke a cigar. The night has been quiet until now.

"I'm on my way to the ER. Have Nurse Boudreaux meet me there. Call in Dr. McClellan, Dr. Hafferty and Dr. Elam. They are all close by, and can be here quickly. I'll triage the patients and make sure the anesthesiologists have the patients ready as soon as they arrive."

***

"Yes, sir." Nurse Jenkins makes the appropriate calls and all of the doctors confirm they will be here as soon as they can. If these trauma situations keep up, the hospital will have to go back on double rotations. Due to budget cuts, it was decided that only one doctor needs to be here at night. Like people only get sick from six in the morning to six at night. She never understood that reasoning.

***

As the ambulance arrives at the hospital, Ty is coming to. The last thing he remembers is leaving the bar and asking a guy if he wanted to drag race. He tries to remember what happened. He keeps drawing a blank on how he ended up on this gurney.

"Sir, please you need to stay lying down. You can't get up just yet."

Ty hears someone talking to him, but he has trouble understanding what he is saying, "Huh? What did you say man?" He knows the man is talking, but it sounds like incoherent babble. What the hell?

"Sir, please stay still. I'm a paramedic. We just arrived at the hospital."

* * *

I hear the sirens as the first ambulance pulls into the bay and I meet them outside. The paramedic opens the double doors as soon as they park, "Doctor, I have two of your patients and the other two are right behind me. One is waking up and trying to move. The young girl is still unconscious. The other two are in bad shape and may not make it at all. One flat lined on the way here."

"I understand it was a bad accident?"

"Yes sir, it was. The State Trooper believes two of the cars involved were drag racing and their speeds were probably around seventy to eighty miles an hour when they hit the other car. The driver of the other car is the one that has flat lined. Two more passengers were thrown from a car and pronounced dead at the scene."

They are moving Ty on a gurney. When he tries to sit up, a nurse forces him back down. The paramedic informs Nurse Jenkins, "We may have to restrain him."

Nurse Jenkins looks over at me, "Is that okay?"

"Just do it. We don't need him walking all over the hospital, dripping blood everywhere." From the looks of the young man and the way he is incoherent when he speaks I suspect it is more than a laceration on his forehead and a banged up face. "After you get him strapped down have CT come pick him up for a scan. I want to make sure there are no head injuries before we sedate him. We need to keep the cervical collar on him, too, just in case he has a neck injury."

No more than one half hour passed before the radiologist calls to inform me that my young patient suffered only a minor concussion and wouldn't need surgery. This was devastating news because I had such plans for him. I can't believe I lost this opportunity. This young man is extremely lucky.

Chapter 9

Dr. Mason Reed has been the Department Head of the surgical committee for the last two years. Thankfully, it has been a relatively quiet two years other than the mandatory scheduled peer reviews. With Mr. Hebert's recent death, no one is sure which department the fault lies with. It could be orthopedics, nursing or surgery. The cause of the MRSA virus has yet to be determined.

Dr. Reed is reviewing Mr. Hebert's charts to familiarize himself with the care he received while here. Larry Stevens is wasting no time asking that all material be reviewed. Even though it is still too early for a lawyer to be involved, no chances are being taken. No one wants to be caught off guard.

Dr. Reed was chosen by the Board of Directors for this position because he is an outsider, brought in to be objective. They knew that he would be totally impartial, knowledgeable and honest. Dr. Reed moved down to Louisiana so that his wife could be closer to her family. After living up north for the last decade, she was ready to move back home. Truth be told, Dr. Reed is ready to relax. He will be sixty years old this year and wants to spend more time with his beloved wife.

Larry Stevens knocks before entering, out of courtesy, "Have you finished your review?"

"I still have to bring it before the committee, but I have reviewed Dr. Habersham's work, and his documentation of the surgery is impeccable. It all looks cut and dry. This will be a difficult case review though. I don't know where the fault lies, if any. Mr. Hebert could have contracted MRSA from the accident scene itself, or even the ambulance. The work done here at the hospital seems to have been top notch. Dr. Cole listened to the patient's complaints and responded accordingly. He did an outstanding job, and was quick on his feet when diagnosis of MRSA was made. Dr. Habersham, as always, did an excellent job in the OR. As of now, no actions will be taken on the matter."

Larry Stevens informs Dr. Reed, "Everyone has been put on notice. All we can do is wait and see if we are contacted by a medical malpractice attorney."

"My initial findings stand; that the treatment Mr. Hebert received here met the acceptable standard of care for this patient. Dr. Habersham and Dr. Cole both did what any reasonable physician would do under the circumstances. I will arrange for a peer review from the surgical committee to make sure we all come to the same conclusion. I would suggest the same from the other committees. Let's make sure all the "i's" are dotted and "t's" are crossed."

"Thank you Dr. Reed." "Glad to help. Once the committees have a final decision I will let you know."

Larry knows that the actions the committees could take range from a slap on the wrist to revocation of hospital privileges. All peer review activities carried out under the hospital committee are exempt from legal discovery. There has always been, and most likely always will be, complaints from lawyers regarding this decision. This protects any doctor from having what he says in front of a peer review committee being used against him in either a civil or criminal case.

Chapter 10

When Drew Hornsby left for work this morning the weather forecast was calling for a sunny day in the high eighty's. Several service calls had come in this afternoon, causing him to work late. It has been a long day, and now he is wishing he hadn't ridden his motorcycle to work. Especially now that he has walked outside and found that it is storming. So much for the weather forecast. Why can't these weathermen get their shit together? How can they be this wrong about the weather? And to top it off, he didn't bring his rain gear with him. This day has sucked since he got to work.

He sends his wife a text letting her know he is leaving work now and will be home soon; that it is raining so he will take it slow. Once he gets onto Highway 14 he opens the motorcycle wide open and cruises home. Unfortunately, the car pulling out never looks to make sure no one is coming. She plows right into him, dragging his motorcycle underneath her SUV for at least a mile before she realizes there are sparks following behind her. Drew is getting ready to find out just how well these leathers he bought take a beating. Thankfully, she didn't drag him the whole way, just his bike. His bike is toast, but at least he has insurance on it. Damn drivers, they never seem to watch out for motorcycles. At least he is alive. If only he could say the same thing for his bike.

The leg that was drug along the road is battered. His knee is in bad shape. He hears the ambulances coming and tries to sit up, but is too dizzy to move. Man, he hopes there is nothing seriously wrong with him.

The ambulance abruptly stops right behind him. He hears the medic talking to him, "Sir, I need you to lie still until we evaluate you. I need to make sure nothing is broken."

He feels the paramedic tugging at his helmet. "My neck, please stop it hurts."

The paramedic stops to access the damage, feeling his neck for any subtle hints and he finds it. There seems to be a knot at the base of the skull.   He yells to his partner, "John I need the back board and collar. Looks like we may have a broken neck here."

Drew hears the medics talking and his worst fears are confirmed. His mom has always told him he will eventually wind up breaking his neck and it looks like she was right. The paramedic looks down at him, "Okay sir, we are going to make sure your back and neck are supported until we get you to the hospital. They will be able to tell how serious your injuries are. We are getting ready to load you into the ambulance. Are you ready?" Drew tries to give him a thumbs-up, but is having difficulty moving his fingers.

***

On the way to the hospital the medics call the accident in to St. Anne's Hospital, "On our way with a motorcycle accident. Possible broken neck and a broken leg and superficial injuries. Luckily, the driver was wearing a helmet and a thick pair of leathers, kept the injuries from being worse than they are."

Nurse Jenkins calls me. "I am still in the hospital. I just finished with another surgery. I'll head on down to the emergency room and meet the patient at the bay doors."

The paramedics are unloading the patient from the ambulance as I am walking outside. "Dr. Habersham, we seem to be keeping you busy lately."

"Yeah, as much as I love operating, I could go back to the slow days for a while. These budget cuts seem to keep us busier than usual, with so few doctors on call now."

I see this accident as a perfect opportunity for another experiment. The leg injury is a chance for me to cut the tendon in the knee. The patellar tendon is the tendon that connects the bottom of the kneecap to the top part of the shin bone. This tendon aids in the proper flexion and extension of the knee. Along with the other ligaments, tendons, muscles and bones of the knee joint, the patellar tendon supports the knee and is essential in the proper movement of the joint. Some of the possible scenarios resulting from this experiment could be the patient may not regain normal levels of function in the knee and a decrease in strength when using the joint, or stiffness in the knee that prevents full range of motion. Permanent loss of motion, joint contractures, weakness and stiffness may be unavoidable.

***

Melanie has never been this scared. She swears she aged ten years when the police officer showed up at her residence to inform her that her husband had been in an accident. She barely remembers driving to the hospital. It is all hazy, but the trauma surgeon promised Dale will be all right. The orthopedic surgeon should be in to talk to them soon about what to expect in the weeks to come.

Melanie tries to wake Drew one more time. She just wants him to open his eyes so that she knows he is okay. "Come on, Drew, just open your eyes for me once. I want to see those gorgeous blues of yours. I promise I'll let you go back to sleep afterwards."

***

Drew hears his wife calling his name, but he doesn't want to wake up. He is so tired.

It takes Drew a couple more minutes to open his eyes. The bright light bothers him. When he opens his eyes, he realizes he is lying in a hospital bed with IV tubes in his arm, a leg in traction and his family surrounding him. His mom has tears in her eyes. *What the hell happened? Why am I here?* Then he begins to remember bits and pieces. It was raining when he left work. A car never stopped and hit his motorcycle, dragging him. Drew doesn't think there is one part of his body that doesn't hurt.

He hears Melanie talking to him. "Drew, do you remember what happened?"

His mouth is extremely dry, "Water."

Carefully putting the straw in his mouth she gives him a small sip of water from a cup.

After his mouth doesn't feel like cotton anymore, he tries speaking again. "I was in an accident."

"Yes, that's right. While you were on your way home from work last night. The cops said the car never stopped, claiming not to see the motorcycle."

"How bad is the bike?"

"It is totaled. The vehicle drug the motorcycle for at least a mile."

"My leg really hurts."

"Your leg was trapped between the bike and road before you could free yourself."

"I can't move my neck."

"You are in traction. At first they thought you had broken your neck, but it is severely bruised. The doctor wants to relieve some of the pressure on your neck until the swelling goes down."

As Melanie is talking, a doctor walks into the room, "Mr. Hornsby, it's good to see you awake. My name is Dr. Jeffrey Cole. I'm your orthopedist. Your leg was severely damaged in the accident. You were wise in buying those leather pants. They helped keep the damage from being far worse.

A trauma surgeon, Dr. Habersham, did the initial operation. A rod was placed in your leg, as well as several plates and screws holding your ankle together. Numerous surgical staples have been placed to hold the skin together along with sutures. The staples will be removed in a few days and the sutures will dissolve in about a week. It will be about a year before the remaining hardware in your leg is removed, depending on how well your leg heals."

"What about work?"

"It will be at least three months before I can release you for work. It is going to depend on how well your leg is healing."

Drew knows that they can't survive with him not working for that long, and he starts to worry. As much as he hates thinking of suing another individual, maybe they should talk to a personal injury attorney and see if there is something that can be done.

As soon as the doctor leaves the room, Drew asks his family if they can give him and Melanie a little time to themselves. "Melanie, we need to have a serious discussion. We can't survive without me working for that long. I need you to talk to a personal injury attorney for me. See if there is something they can do to help us."

"Drew, are you sure about this? I can ask mom and dad for some help. I can always go back to work."

"Melanie, we need to look into this. The medical bills will be astronomical. The health insurance company will not cover all the expenses. The split is seventy/thirty this year, remember?"

"If that's what you want, I'll make some calls."

"It's not what I want, but it is what needs to be done, and fast."

***

Melanie Hornsby goes through attorneys listed in the yellow pages and finds that the law office of Barry LeVoux is just two blocks from the hospital.

When she calls, Mr. LeVoux informs her that he can meet with her that afternoon. His ad in the phonebook states he handles personal injury cases, including slip and falls and motor vehicle accidents. Melanie hopes he isn't some kind of shyster.

***

When Barry LeVoux takes Melanie's call he is intrigued. He loves these types of personal injury cases. This one is cut and dry from what Melanie stated. The insurance company will probably settle as soon as he informs them he is representing Drew Hornsby. He is anxious to see what kind of limits the driver carried on her policy. But there is no way it will be enough to cover all the damages Mr. Hornsby will have. He will need to look into other avenues.

When his receptionist buzzes him to announce his new client's arrival, he walks up to the front desk to greet her. She rushes to him with her hand extended, "Mr. LeVoux, thank you for agreeing to meet me so quickly."

"No problem at all, Mrs. Hornsby. Let's go to my office to discuss this matter."

As he closes his office door, Mrs. Hornsby takes a seat. After he sits down at his desk he says, "Let me start off by telling you how sorry I am for you and your husband. I know this is a difficult time for the both of you. I want you to know I will do everything in my power to help you through this tragedy."

Melanie has tears welling up, "Thank you."

"I will need to meet with your husband. He needs to sign the retainer and medical releases. Once I have the records, I will contact the insurance company and put them on notice. I honestly don't believe I will have to file a lawsuit. I look for them to settle pretty quickly. I must warn you that there probably won't be enough money to cover all of Drew's lost wages, medical bills and so on. I plan on getting full policy limits from them. I would also like to review your policy for the motorcycle, to see if you have medical payment coverage and underinsured."

"I'm pretty sure we do. Our insurance is through one company. Drew's mom begged him to get the max he could on his insurance policy. She didn't like it when he purchased the motorcycle, and she pressured him to make sure he was at least well insured, just in case something happened to him when riding."

"Excellent. If you can bring me in the policy, I will check to make sure."

"Yes sir, I can. How much is this going to cost us?"

"My usual retainer is twenty- five percent before litigation. If I have to go to court, then I usually charge thirty-three percent. However, in your unfortunate situation, I plan on dropping my fee to twenty percent regardless. Once we have a settlement, I will deduct my expenses and fees from the amount and cut you a check. I will try and pressure the insurance company to pay my fees and expenses on top of the settlement amount. I plan on seeing if the defendant has any personal assets we can also go after."

"I don't know. Something about suing an individual seems wrong to me."

"Look at it this way, that individual didn't stop to think about dragging your husband behind their car did they?"

"No, I suppose you are right."

"Besides, they may not have any assets we can go after. Only time will tell."

"Well, okay then. When do you want to go and talk to Drew?"

***

After they make plans to meet at the hospital later on, Melanie goes to grab a quick bite to eat. Her anxiety about talking to a lawyer is fading. Maybe this is the right thing to do.

***

Barry LeVoux is meeting Mr. and Mrs. Hornsby in the hospital at five o'clock. His secretary has printed out all the releases and forms that need to be signed, as well as changing the contingency fee amount to a straight twenty percent.

"Mrs. Hornsby, good to see you again."

Melanie turns and introduces him to Drew. "Drew, this is Barry LeVoux."

Barry's smile spreads impossibly wide across his face when he sees his future client lying in the hospital bed. "It's a pleasure to meet you Mr. Hornsby." This case is better than he imagined. If only he could show the jury pictures of him now. Actually, that may not be a bad idea.

"Call me Drew please."

"Yes sir. Drew, would you mind if I take a few pictures of you for my files?" Barry LeVoux already has the letter planned out in his head that he will send to the insurance company. He will make sure to include photos of his client to help seal the deal.

"I suppose not."

Somehow he has to find more insurance coverage. Once the pictures are taken Barry LeVoux gets down to business.

"Drew, I brought in some papers for you to sign. I already explained to your wife that due to your injuries and the possible lack of insurance coverage, I will reduce my contingency fee to twenty percent. This first document is the retainer agreement outlining the financial arrangements. The next one is a medical records release. It allows me to get the appropriate medical records so that I can forward those to the insurance company. This will help me show them what injuries the carelessness of their driver caused to you."

Drew looks over the papers thoroughly before signing. Barry LeVoux knows this is money in the bank. He has also been making some inquiries about the lady who hit his client, she is loaded.

Chapter 11

Bud Ramos has finally talked Sherry Lambert into going out with him. All the guys on the football team have talked about how easy she is, so there has to be something wrong with him. He has had no luck getting any action from her yet. Hell, he even brought her to Springport for supper and a movie, thinking that would sweeten the deal. He has spent all his money on this one date. What the crap?

They are on Highway 14 on their way back to Hope, and he's hoping to talk her into pulling over for a bit of action. He has to give it another shot. "I know a little place off the road if you want to take a small detour before we get home."

*****

Sherry knows what he wants, but her dad threatened her that if she misses her curfew tonight he will take her car away from her. "I can't tonight. My dad will kill me if I'm late again. I didn't know we would be going all the way to Springport or I would have asked him for later curfew."

"Come on Sherry, you can be a little late can't you? Call and tell him the movie ran later than you thought."

"I can't take a chance. There is no way I want to be stuck at my house without any wheels."

"Sherry, you are killing me. I was hoping we could have some fun tonight."

"What's to say we can't still have a little fun?"

Looking around, Sherry makes sure that there aren't any cars around. She's heard about other girls doing this because they weren't ready to lose their virginity. It can't be that big of a deal, maybe just a little uncomfortable. "How adventurous are you feeling tonight?"

"What do you have in mind?"

Sherry strokes his jeans, getting a rise out of him pretty fast.

"Oh man, Sherry, you are teasing me now."

"I've heard from some of my friends that this is something you will really like."

Sherry unbuckles her seatbelt so she can get closer to him.

"What exactly are you planning on doing?"

Sherry smiles with a mischievous grin in her eyes, "Something you won't forget for a very long time. Just keep your eyes on the road and enjoy."

Sherry unzips his jeans so she can have better access to him. "You might have to help me out a little."

Bud arranges his jeans until his hard on is out of his boxers. He is expecting her to give him a hand job, but she takes him into her mouth. He swerves from the sheer surprise of her bold move.

Sherry stops what she is doing and looks at him. "I don't want to get killed on the way home, eyes on the road."

"But you won't have any enjoyment, just me. Take off your panties so I can at least touch you." With a little shifting of bodies they are both getting off, and never see the eighteen-wheeler ahead of them. Bud drives underneath the massive truck, completely shearing off the top of his car, along with his head. The impact of the accident forces Sherry to be pinned between the steering wheel and the lower half of Bud's body.

***

When the medics arrive at the scene of the accident, it takes them by surprise. They thought the driver of the eighteen wheeler was exaggerating when he said that a car was stuck under his trailer. It takes a while for them to free the car; they get an even bigger surprise once they look inside. This is one accident that will be talked about for a long time.

It will take time to extract the young girl who is pinned to the front seat. It appears as if her head is actually caught in the steering wheel.

"Miss, we are going to try and get you out as fast as we can, but please try not to move. I need you to stay as calm as possible." The medic isn't sure of the extent of her injuries. There is so much blood. And due to the injuries that the boy sustained, he isn't sure if some could belong to the young girl or not. He can hear her moaning, so she is at least alive and conscious. The fire department is using the jaws of life to extract her from the car.

One fireman still can't believe the scene, "I've worked some strange accidents, but I must say this is a first for me." The medic agrees with him.

Once she has been freed, the medics begin to help her.

"Miss, we need to check on you before we can move you. Please stay still a little longer."

Her facial injuries are very extensive, and she is rushed off to the emergency room. The medics alert the hospital en route. "Our ETA is approximately ten minutes. The young girl has extensive facial lacerations, possible broken nose and jaw. I would suggest a trauma surgeon be on standby."

Nurse Jenkins is taken aback for a moment, "I will call Dr. Habersham immediately."

* * *

I answer the hospital's call on the second ring. I have just started dozing off in the on call room. "Dr. Habersham, we have a MVA victim en route to the ER. She suffered facial lacerations as well as a possible broken nose and jaw."

"The medic informed me she was awake at the scene, and coherent. "

"I'm on my way down." Even if the injuries aren't as serious as the medic believes, it is something that I want to witness first hand.

I enter the emergency room as the medics arrive, and appraise her injuries. The medic was correct in his assessment that she will need trauma surgery. What she really needs though is a plastic surgeon. Unfortunately, St.

Anne's does not have one on staff. Her jaw and nose are shattered, as well as several facial bones. It will be a long reconstructive surgery. The best we can do is stabilize her and transport her to a hospital that does have a plastic surgeon on call.

I instruct the triage nurse, "Call around and find out which hospital we can transfer her to once she is stabilized."

"Yes doctor."

The medics help wheel her into the trauma room. You can see the fear in the young girl's eyes. Her blond hair is matted with blood from the accident. When I look down at this mutilated face I think of all of the experiments I could perform on her. The possibilities are endless. For the first one, I read where a young surgeon accidentally punctured the brain casing with an instrument during routine nasal surgery, resulting in a serious brain injury. This may be something I have to recreate to see if it is actually possible. The next is cutting a tendon in her jaw; that is if one isn't cut already. I love experiments involving cut tendons or removing a bone.

The medics transfer the young girl, who is strapped to a hardboard stretcher to keep her neck stabilized during transport, from the stretcher to the gurney. I step back and let the nurses do their duty. They need to take the girl's vitals, start an IV, draw blood, clean some of the blood off her injuries, and strip off her remaining clothes.

Nurse Boudreaux is explaining to the young girl what is happening, "I need to cut your clothes off. You need to be still a little bit longer."

The girl blinks rapidly and moans, but keeps still as her clothes are being cut off. She is wearing a short skirt so the only difficult item to remove is the shirt. I noticed she was wearing no underwear, which fits with the medic's story of the accident. Due to the injuries she has sustained to her jaw, she is unable to talk, just moan. There is no way they will be able to get an accurate medical history from her. The police officer working the scene sent a patrol car to her parents' house, but as of yet, no one has come to the hospital.

Next I order that x-rays be taken. We need to see how bad her facial fractures are, and check for chest trauma or laceration of an organ. The x-ray technician moves the portable x-ray machine over to the patient. Once it is in place he asks everyone to clear the room except for one female nurse, who has been provided with a lead apron. Several x-rays are taken. It is taking quite a while, since it is difficult to move the patient, the x-ray machine had to be repositioned.

I am getting impatient at the amount of time it is taking to get the girl prepped for surgery, "Where the hell are my x-rays?"

The tech rushes into the room with the films, "Here!" He quickly places them on the viewing box. The x-rays confirm that the patient has several fractured ribs, but no other serious injuries have been noticed involving the chest or abdomen. She can be prepped for surgery. Her rib fractures aren't life-threatening by any means, but they will be extremely painful. At this point it is too early to rule out a brain injury, but for now it does not appear she has received one. No damage to the spinal cord and neck are noted. Once the patient has been anesthetized and the bleeding from her face is controlled, surgery can begin. A CT scan has also been performed to show the extent of the injuries. This poor girl will have a massive amount of hardware in her face until she can be seen by a plastic surgeon.

I instruct the nurse to get a catheter in so that we can begin. Nurse Boudreaux does a quick prep, parts her labia and slides in the Foley. "Dr. Habersham, there is blood in the urine."

"Shit, she probably has a ruptured bladder also." Upon examination of the pelvic area, I confirm that it is bruised and seems to be ballooning up rather quickly.

"Did we x-ray the kidneys?"

"Yes sir, the kidneys are fine."

"Well, let's do a cystogram and check the bladder, stat."

X-ray dye is inserted into the Foley catheter. The x-ray reveals the dye running straight up into the abdomen. "She has a ruptured bladder. We need to open her belly, and repair it."

Nurse Boudreaux grimaces. "That will take a lot more time. She might go into shock before we can finish."

"We'll be fine. I plan on moving quickly. Get another intern down here, one you trust. He can learn from this experience." I also know that an intern will know better than to question anything I may do, if he even noticed something out of the ordinary.

"Yes doctor." Nurse Boudreaux asks for an intern to head to trauma stat. She still isn't familiar with the newest group of interns, but there has to be one willing to help with the surgery.

It didn't take long for two interns to arrive. I instruct Nurse Boudreaux to let them both in. This is a learning experience for both of the young interns. "Have either of you worked on a ruptured bladder?"

"No doctor."

"Damn, well then you can at least assist so that we can get this girl stabilized quicker."

Her face has been wrapped in gauze extremely well and will wait until the internal injuries are taken care of. Nurses and orderlies gather up the lines, IV poles and move the gurney into the OR. Nurse Boudreaux can see the fear in the girl's eyes, "You are going to be alright. Dr. Habersham is one of the best. You have nothing to worry about."

I merely look at her and ask, "Have her parents arrived yet?"

"They just arrived. Nurse Jenkins is having them sign the consent forms as we speak."

"Did we get a history?"

"No major illnesses or surgeries. The girl's father is demanding to see her."

"Tell Nurse Jenkins that he will be able to see her once the surgery is complete, but I need to act fast. I wouldn't give too many details right now, but she can let them know there are serious facial fractures and lacerations as well as a ruptured bladder. What about allergies?"

"None noted."

"She may need a blood transfusion. Has she been cross-matched?"

"The lab is backed up. I'm waiting on the results."

"We don't have the time. Let's go universal donor, O-negative. We need the blood now to get started. It can take a while for the lab to cross-match and we don't have the time."

Nurse Boudreaux calls down to the blood bank, "We need five units of O-negative blood stat."

As soon as the young girl is wheeled into the OR, the anesthesiologist gets busy hooking up the leads for the heart monitor, blood pressure cuff and a temperature probe.

I pull up my mask, make sure the scrubs are cinched, and state, "Let's get this operation started." I look over at the anesthesiologist and ask, "We good to go?"

He confirms, "Ready on my end."

A thin ribbon of blood follows the knife down her belly. To avoid damaging the bladder any further, the incision curves around the belly button, then straight down to just above the pubis. Once the abdominal cavity is opened, I can see clearly that urine and blood fill the area.

I instruct one intern, "Moisten the sponges with saline to gently pull the bowel out of the way."

Nurse Boudreaux is as efficient as ever. She has all the instruments laid out with precision. No matter what personal differences we may have, we work together seamlessly in the OR. She knows what I will need next without me saying a word. She also seems to be the only nurse on staff that isn't bothered by my aggressive personality. She merely tunes out the yelling and cursing I do in the OR and does her job.

After some extensive exploration, I find the hole in the bladder. Clamps are quickly passed and placed on either side of the lacerated bladder so that the repairs can be made. A nurse hangs another bag of blood, but the bleeding seems to be under control. I perform a quick inspection of the spleen, pancreas and liver to make sure there is no bleeding from them. All look good.

Looking at one intern, I instruct him, "Shoot some saline through the Foley so I can confirm that the bladder is repaired."

"Yes, doctor."

Once the internal repairs are made, I have the interns close up the incision and I move on to the girl's face. This will be even more time consuming than stopping the internal bleeding. "It looks like this will be a very long surgery ladies and gentlemen. Let's keep the momentum going though."

It is easy to puncture a tiny hole in the brain casing while repairing her nose. The best part of this experiment is that the injury will be blamed on the accident. She will most likely have a small amount of drainage from one or both nostrils. This will be due to cerebral-spinal fluid draining from the brain into the sinuses. There is a high chance the patient will get an infection, such as meningitis. Meningitis can affect the nervous system and can even be life-threatening, only time will tell. Unfortunately, I did not get to cut the tendon in her jaw; the accident did that for me. However, I elected not to repair the damage before wiring her jaw shut. There is a chance that due to the jaw healing with the tendon not repaired it will be misaligned. There is always a possibility that the plastic surgeon will notice and fix the tendon.

Chapter 12

Jacob Lambert fears his world is coming to end when the police officer knocks on his door and informs him that his daughter has been involved in a car accident. As he and his wife, Miranda, rush off to the hospital, all he can think about is being hard on his daughter that day. He has been riding her case really hard lately, and now he can't remember the last time he actually told her he loved her. He doesn't want the last memory his daughter has of him to be that he was disappointed in her.

He rushes up to the receptionist at the ER desk, "My name is Jacob Lambert. I was told my daughter, Sherry, was brought to the emergency room. She was in a car accident.

"Mr. Lambert if you will have a seat I will let the charge nurse know that you are here."

Nurse Jenkins rushes out to talk to them. "Mr. Lambert, I'm Nurse Jenkins. The doctor is getting ready to operate on your daughter and we need your consent to do so. There is no easy way to say this, but she has severe facial injuries."

"Is she awake?"

"Yes, sir. Her injuries are quite severe though, and Dr. Habersham is getting ready to operate. I have the consent forms here for you to sign. As soon as I know something I will come and let you know."

"She is going to be okay though?"

"I won't know more until they operate, but I do know she will require some follow-up care. She may need to be transferred to a hospital where a plastic surgeon is available, but we need to get her stabilized for that to happen. Dr. Habersham is the trauma surgeon performing the operation. He is one of the best surgeons we have. Your daughter is in excellent hands."

"Where do I need to sign?"

Jacob paces the floor as he waits for any news regarding his daughter's condition. Jacob is over six feet tall and at one time had a muscular frame. Age has started to catch up with him though and his once full head of hair has begun to thin and turn gray. His weight has started to climb, which he tries to ignore. His doctor keeps telling him to lose about fifty pounds, which is always easier said than done.

With each passing hour his apprehension grows. His wife is sitting in a far corner of the waiting room saying the rosary. He takes a seat next to her and holds her hand tightly. She gives his hand a squeeze back and looks at him with tears in her eyes. "She's going to be alright, isn't she?"

Jacob isn't sure he can answer her without the fear coming through in his voice, "I'm praying that she is. This surgeon is supposed to be really good."

The waiting room seems to be full tonight. Jacob wonders how many are seeking treatment and how many are waiting for news just like them. With all the people in the small room it is getting uncomfortably hot. They really should turn the air conditioner down some. They could at least make those of us that are waiting more comfortable. The heat is mixing with the foul smell of illness that seems to fill the room, along with the stench emanating from some of those waiting. The smell is making him nauseas; his nerves are already strung tight. Although he isn't sure if it is the odor or his nerves making him feel ill. His stomach is turning violently and he doubts anything will calm it.

With his patience finally exhausted, he walks up to the receptionist desk once again, "Have you at least heard if she is still in surgery?"

The triage looks at him sympathetically, "I haven't heard anything, but let me call the OR and see if there is any news."

The triage nurse asks the OR nurse who answered the phone if Dr. Habersham is still in surgery, "They are still operating on the patient. I actually have not seen anyone exit yet."

"Thanks, the dad was wondering."

She informs Mr. Lambert, "They are still in surgery, sir. I promise you once they are done someone will be down here to talk to you. I know you are anxious, but Dr. Habersham is wonderful. He will take good care of your daughter."

Jacob looks around the hospital, trying to take his mind off of his daughter's surgery. There are stretchers pushed along the wall, abandoned by the medical care providers, who are rushing off to save patients' lives. The triage nurse is desperately trying to keep up with the influx of people rushing in. A young man has a towel wrapped around his hand, trying to contain the flow of blood, and at the other end of the ER waiting room is a young woman leaning over a trash can vomiting violently. No matter where he looks he sees despair and hopelessness. He tries to reach down deep inside himself and find some sympathy for those working here tonight, but he is getting impatient waiting for news on his daughter. Unfortunately, compassion was never an emotion he had much of.

Out of the corner of his eye, he notices the triage nurse walking towards him, "Mr. and Mrs. Lambert, if you will please follow me to the consultation room, the nurse will be right down to talk to you. Dr. Habersham is finishing up with your daughter."

They follow the nurse in silence, praying that the news is good. Jacob Lambert can't remember the last time he prayed this much. He would give anything to trade places with his little girl.

The small consultation room is sparse and looks like it may have once been an office. There is a couch and a desk with chairs situated in front of the desk. No other furniture is in the room.

"Please have a seat. Nurse Boudreaux will be here shortly."

As Nurse Boudreaux enters the room, both parents are pacing back and forth, "Mr. and Mrs. Lambert, please have a seat."

Jacob Lambert looks directly at her, "Please, just tell us how she is."

"Your daughter's operation went as smooth as it could under the circumstances. Her condition is stabilized, and we will transfer her in the morning to N'Awlins Heritage. They have a top notch plastic surgeon there that will begin reconstructing her face."

"How bad is it?"

"Your daughter unfortunately suffered severe facial fractures. Her nose, jaw and cheekbones will all have to be reconstructed. Dr. Habersham did the best he could, but it is not enough. We just don't have the services here that she needs."

"Can we at least see her?"

"She will be taken to ICU soon. You can wait there, and I'm sure the charge nurse will let you see her once they get her settled in. But, I must warn you that it is not a pretty sight. Please remember that she is swollen and bandaged from the surgery."

All Jacob Lambert cares about is making sure his daughter is alive.

Chapter 13

Travis Mitchell has enjoyed visiting his cousins and friends in Springport for the day. He is getting ready to leave for Army boot camp, and this is the last day he can spend with everyone. They decide to go play a game of basketball in the park. As soon as they begin, though, another group of boys arrives, wanting the court. They attempt to bully Travis and his friends into leaving. What starts out as a verbal argument, soon escalates into physical violence. A boy in the other group pulls a knife on Travis. The boy lunges toward Travis with the knife and takes aim at his chest. Travis tries to defend himself from the attack, but it is too late. He feels a stabbing pain in his chest as he collapses to the ground. He feels two more sharp pains as the boy continues to stab him in the chest and hand. The last thing Travis remembers is hearing sirens in the distance.

Within minutes the cops arrive. They ask the witnesses if they saw which direction the attacker or attackers took off in.

"They headed down the street towards the back of the old school." said one of Travis's friends.

Soon after, the paramedics arrive. They place Travis on a stretcher and leave for St. Anne's Hospital. They report the patient's status along with their ETA to the dispatcher. As the paramedics are leaving, another patrol car pulls up to help work the crime scene, and interview the witnesses.

Even with the victim having sustained multiple stab wounds to the chest and his hand, the medic notes that Travis is awake and alert throughout the entire transport.

***

When they arrive at the hospital, Travis is moved from the stretcher onto a hospital gurney. The only complaint he has is shortness of breath. The emergency room doctor observes that Travis does indeed have decreased breath sounds at the left base. The chest x-ray confirms a left sided hemopneumothorax.

Travis begins complaining of pain between his shoulder blades. The attending orders blood work, just to be on the safe side, and calls the trauma surgeon on call, Dr. Habersham. Patients with diaphragmatic injuries and irritation from the blood frequently exhibit referred pain between their shoulder blades. If the knife wound has penetrated the diaphragm, there is also a high likelihood of intra-abdominal injuries. Dr. Habersham confirms that Travis requires exploratory surgery, and he is taken to the operating room.

***

Once I have the patient opened, I find the obvious defect in the diaphragm. Inspection within the abdomen demonstrates blood clots on the anterior surface of the stomach, and the left lateral segment of the liver. There are three lacerations on the surface of the liver which require suture closure. There is also a 2 centimeter perforation of the anterior surface of the stomach which I close using two layers of sutures. I then proceed to close the diaphragmatic perforation and repair the pneumothorax injury.

While examining the lung, I make an unexpected discovery, the tip of the knife. It must have broken off after hitting a bone during the attack. I quickly decide to leave it in place. I'm not sure what complications will arise from this experiment, but it will be intriguing to see what happens.

Chapter 14

After four years of studying at the University of Louisiana, Denise Duplantis, D.D. for short, is ready to graduate. Finals are next week and she has been hitting the books at least twelve hours a day. She has been living off of energy drinks and coffee. Tonight, though, she and her friends have decided to meet up at a local bar and unwind.

Her degree is in general studies, and she still isn't sure what she wants to do with her life. After living in the apartments in Springport for the last four years she is seriously considering moving back to her hometown, Hope, Louisiana. Growing up, she couldn't wait to get out of the small town, especially after the serial killer terrorized the town a while back, but now she has come to realize that city life may not be for her. She had just as much fun growing up there as she did partying here with her friends. Except here the crime rate seems to be a lot higher.

The only problem is there are very few jobs in Hope where she can earn a decent salary. Her parents keep reminding her that money isn't everything. She just isn't sure what she wants to do. Hopefully it will come to her before graduation. She has started scanning the help wanted ads, but hasn't really actively pursued finding a job.

D.D. looks at the clock and decides she had best get dressed if she wants to meet her friends on time. She looks at herself in the mirror and scowls in frustration. This humidity is not helping her hair today. She looks as if she stuck her finger in an electrical socket. Using some anti-frizz gel she tries to style her hair into submission. Her hair does not want to cooperate though. It is not even close to being manageable tonight. The only possible solution in the short amount of time she has is to put in in a ponytail.

Looking into the mirror, she gives herself a once over to make sure she looks presentable. With all the studying she has been doing, she hasn't been eating like she should and notices she has lost weight, although with all the coffee and energy drinks she has been consuming she hasn't been hungry. Maybe she can start a new fad diet, the caffeine diet.

As she applies her makeup, she realizes that her face is pale. Her eyes also seem to be a little shallower than before, and no matter how hard she tries she can't hide the dark circles. She's not too worried though because she knows the rest of her friends have the same problems. Once finals are over with she will be able to put some color back into her skin. Maybe she can talk a few friends into renting a condo on the beach and relax a few days before entering the real world.

As D.D. goes into her room to finish getting dressed, she sees that Amy, one of her roommates, is asleep on the couch. Earlier that day, Amy had told D.D. that she was too tired to go out and party. She wants to catch up on some sleep. Amy still has another year of school, and has already told D.D. she will take over the lease if D.D. moves out. Available apartments this close to the college campus are scarce; and Amy doesn't want to chance not finding another place to stay. She still isn't sure what she wants to do. There are lots of jobs available in Springport; it's such a difficult decision. Stay here, or move back home? D.D. isn't sure if she could move back into her parents' house either. They will never allow her to stay out all night. Her dad will want to place a curfew on her. She has enjoyed her freedom these past four years. Not that she stayed out all night every night, but if she wanted to she could.

D.D. notices that the air outside is unseasonably cool. It isn't cool enough for a sweater, but it isn't nearly as hot as she thought it would be. Given that it doesn't look like it is going to rain, and she won't be melting by the time she gets to the bar, she decides to walk. This way she won't have to worry if she drinks too much. She can just stumble back home or catch a cab. The bar is only a couple of blocks away, so she should be fine.   Overhead the full moon is playing peekaboo behind what few clouds there are in the sky. Inhaling deeply she breathes in the night air. She can smell the star jasmine that her landlord has planted in the garden. Even the gardenia bushes are in full bloom and very fragrant tonight.

She walks to the bar on the left side of the road so that she can watch for oncoming traffic. It is starting to get dark outside, but there should be enough light so that drivers will notice her. She packed her heels in her purse so that she can wear her tennis shoes to walk in. She watches as two cars zoom pass her, neither bothering with the posted speed limit. Crazy drivers! When she gets to her first big intersection, she waits for the walk signal. Keeping a careful eye out, she doesn't see anyone turning. The nearest car is not in the turn lane, and looks to be going straight. Suddenly the car changes lanes and hits her. D.D. never has a chance to move out of the car's destructive path. The driver never even hits his brakes, just runs over her and keeps going. The front bumper of the car has mangled her lower extremities. She is fortunate that the car missed her upper torso. The pain from her legs seems to rip through her entire body. Hot blood gushes out of her and spills onto the pavement. She can feel herself losing consciousness and fights to stay awake. Thankfully, her purse is close by. She reaches in to find her phone. She dials 911 and tells the operator what had happened and where she is. The operator is talking to her in a soothing voice, trying to keep her calm and awake. It is difficult, since she is tired and cold.

The mounting terror that the paramedics won't arrive in time occupies her mind. She strains to hear the sirens. A pair of headlights loom in front of her. She waves her hands praying they don't run over her, too. She hears the car stop and the driver get out. "Please help me!"pleads D.D.

"I'm calling 911."

In between agonizing breaths, she states, "I've already called them. Please don't leave me. I don't want to die all alone."

"I'm not going to leave you. I'll stay here with you until the ambulance arrives."

With disbelief in her voice, D.D. sniffles and says, "The car never even stopped."

"Don't worry, the ambulance is here now." The night air is filled with the wailing of the siren. Seconds later the area is lit up with the flashing orange and red strobe lights. The man who stopped to help quickly moves out of the paramedics' way.

One of the medics is busy taking vitals and another is starting up the IV. As soon as they are sure D.D. is stabilized enough for transport she is carefully placed on the collapsible stretcher and wheeled into the ambulance. Before D.D. knows it the ambulance ride is over and she has made it to the hospital.

She is in and out of consciousness, but hears someone say broken pelvic bones and trauma surgery. It isn't long before she stops fighting the overwhelming fatigue and she falls into a deep sleep.

**

The emergency room is buzzing with activity once the ambulance arrives. Nurses, orderlies, lab and x-ray techs surround the patient all at once. Nurse Boudreaux is assessing the patient, while another nurse starts fluids through the IV in the patient's left arm.

The x-ray tech is busy pushing x-ray plates under the girl's legs and hips, being careful not to jostle her too much. Occasionally he yells, "X-ray!" and everyone dashes behind a lead screen that has been set up for just this purpose. Afterwards, everyone rushes back to continue their care of the patient. This goes on for a few minutes until all the necessary films are shot.

Nurse Boudreaux asks Nurse Jenkins, "Do we know if the family has been contacted so that we can get a medical history on the patient. We need to know if she has any allergies, especially to medicine, and if she has had any previous surgeries."

"I haven't heard anything since she arrived. I will check though."

Nurse Boudreaux sees me walk into the room and explains, "Hit and run. She's virtually shattered from the waist down. Looks like he never slowed down when he ran over her."

I look at the mangled patient, "Let's get a Foley catheter started on her."

"Yes doctor."

Nurse Jenkins comes back into the room, "I spoke with the police, and they are still trying to locate a relative. I didn't see anything in her purse that would help. I have a nurse going through her phone right now. We don't have time to wait for them to locate family."

"Good thinking. We also need to get more hands in here. If they aren't busy I want nurses or interns in here stat. We need to get her prepped and up to surgery."

Nurse Boudreaux instructs a nurse, "Let's cut off her clothes. Be careful with the lower half of her body."

Once her clothes are removed, nurses clean the patient as gently as possible. Asphalt and grime have managed to get into some of the deeper cuts. The young woman has several cuts, scrapes and bruises along her upper body as well as the tangled mess of her lower body.

The two nurses that have just joined them have been told it was a hit and run accident, but neither expected anything like this. They pull themselves together quickly, and jump in the middle of the chaos. A nurse from the orthopedic floor has also come down to help. She notices the patient's legs are angled grotesquely, and in some places the flesh and meat have been torn away, revealing bone.

The crunch of bones being moved fills the room. Even with the pain medicine, the patient lets out a loud groan. Now that the legs are straightened the orthopedic nurse feels for a pulse in her ankles and the top of her feet.

The patient is breathing in short, rapid breaths. Her eyes dart back and forth nervously, as if trying to absorb all the activity going on around her. The young woman asks no one in particular, "Am I going to be okay? My legs hurt so bad."

"We are going to take very good care of you. Dr. Habersham over there is one of our best surgeons."

Nurse Boudreaux tries to bring some resemblance of organization to the chaos around the patient. Looking at the lab tech, "Did you get blood drawn? We need to make sure we do a type and cross along with a CBC, lytes and glucose."

"I'm rushing these down to the lab now. I will tell them that this patient is their number one priority."

"Good. What about the Foley? Is that in?"

A nurses yells out, "It's done. We confirmed that there is blood in the urine."

"Okay. Make sure you note that."

I see the x-ray tech enter the room, "Let me see the films."

"Yes, Dr. Habersham." He quickly gets them arranged on the view box. The chest film looks fairly good for someone that has been struck by a car. Possibly one or two fractured ribs, and a collapsed lung.

I instruct Nurse Boudreaux, "We have a collapsed lung here. We need to intubate and get a chest tube in."

Her spine films thankfully show no fracture, but her pelvis is shattered. "The ileum is broken in pieces. Since she has bloody urine we need to check her kidneys with an IVP stat."

The x-ray dye is injected into the IV and in a matter of minutes they have the results. More x-rays are taken of the abdomen. Looking at the films, "Kidneys are fine. Let's get a cystogram done and check her bladder."

The cystogram confirms that she does indeed have a ruptured bladder. Looking over the x-rays once again, I inform the team, "We need to get her into surgery and take care of her internal injuries. Then we can see if we can salvage her legs."

They immediately prepares her ready to transport to OR.

While the young girl is conscious they get a brief medical history and explain that they need her to sign a consent to operate. Nurse Boudreaux explains the process to her, "We need this before we can operate. We are not sure what will need to be done until they begin. We need to fix your pelvis and stop the internal bleeding. Don't worry though, whatever is wrong Dr. Habersham will fix it, he is the best."

Shaking her head, she signs the consent the best she can.

The anesthesiologist has his work station set up as the patient is brought into the room. Nurse Boudreaux informs him, "We still don't have the type and cross yet."

The anesthesiologist informs her, "I already requested O-negative from the lab. The blood bank is calling around to see how many more O-negatives they can get just in case."

The anesthesiologist states, "I'm ready."

I look around at everyone, "Let's put this young woman back together."

Once the incision is made, the anesthesiologist notices her pressure dropping, "Pressure's down. I'm going to give her some O-negative blood."

A circulating nurse hangs another bag of blood while the anesthesiologist hooks up the CVP, central venous pressure tubing. "She is on her second bag of O-negative. Heart rate is 130."

The anesthesiologist instructs the circulating nurse, "Call the blood bank and get me some more O-negative. Also, see why they are taking so long with the type and cross. She has a long time before she is done with surgery."

The circulating nurse informs them, "They just had four more units of O-negative delivered and are trying to find more. They are still working on type and cross."

"Tell them to hurry. We don't want to run behind on fluids and take the risk of her going into shock."

Once the internal bleeding is stopped and damage repaired, I move on to setting her pelvic bone. While in there I decide this time instead of removing a bone I will leave a small piece of bone fragment floating around in her body. Now there is a possibility that the bone fragment will soften and be absorbed by the body, but there is also a chance that the bone fragment may shift and move. It may lodge into a nerve or muscle, incapacitating a specific function of the body. It may cause numbness or chronic pain, depending on where it settles.   The possibilities are endless.

Chapter 15

I am getting ready to go home when Larry Stevens, the hospital administrator, asks me to come up to his office before leaving. Now what the hell does that man want?

"Dr. Habersham, thank you for seeing me before you head home."

He must need something, which is the only reason for him to be nice to me. "No problem. Did you need something?"

"You are one of the top surgeons here and our malpractice carrier is asking that we do a lecture on patient safety. I was hoping you would do it for me. You are one of the most senior surgeons here and you have worked at a teaching hospital."

I can't help but think of the irony of this request. "No problem. When do you want to schedule the lecture?"

"How long will you need to prepare?"

"Is three weeks good for you?"

I can see the shock on Larry's face. I'm not sure if he is surprised I agreed to do it, or that it won't take me long to prepare for the lecture. Thanks to the internet and resources I have collected over the years, it won't be hard to prepare for this lecture. Plus the last Continued Learning Educational seminar I attended this past year touched on the same subject. I should have the material from that lecture around my office somewhere.

"If you think you can do it in that time frame that is no problem for me. I must say I thought you would either say no or that it would take at least two months."

We select a day that I am not on call to do the lecture. I spend about three hours beforehand organizing all my information. I may have gone overboard but I even prepared a power point presentation and have handouts for everyone. Larry Stevens has made it a mandatory meeting unless you are tied up on a case. The handouts will show the insurance carrier that the hospital is trying to be as cooperative as possible and even help those that can't attend the lecture.

Looking around it seems as though most of the physicians are here, but I know they would rather be anywhere else. No doctor wants to hear about medical mistakes that a fellow colleague made.

Larry Stevens starts off the lecture by stating, "As you all know we are here because the hospital's malpractice insurance carrier has requested this lecture be held. They have approved the contents of Dr. Habersham's speech, so I won't beat around the bush. I want to remind everyone that you need to sign in at the doors so we can verify attendance. Let's hope we can get through this without any emergencies to pull any of you away."

It was my turn to speak, "I know none of us want to talk about medical mistakes, diagnostic, surgical or otherwise. Unfortunately, it is something that occurs. In this parish alone, there were one thousand deaths attributed to medical errors this past year. That number may not seem high, but we are a rather small parish here in Louisiana.

Thankfully, very few of those errors happened at St. Anne's." I left out that most times it is a physician's arrogance and ambivalence that contributes to the errors, but then that would include me in the equation.

Chapter 16

The number of homeless in Springport is increasing faster than anyone cares to admit. Most of the homeless tend to live downtown, in a dilapidated hotel.

The Regency was once a grand hotel here in Springport. The stately hotel sat on a five acre site that overlooked the majestic Mississippi River. It once housed more than 250 hotel rooms, two swimming pools, parking spaces and the convention center. Several movie stars were known to stay there when filming in the area. Back in 1972 the presidential suite was said to go for $150 a night and the regular rooms started at $70. A massive crystal chandelier hung above the black-and-white, marble-tiled lobby, and antique and French provincial furniture sets the standard in affluence.   At the far end of the hotel was a grand building, which had several ballrooms and other rooms available that could be rented out for weddings and other events. The hotel exuded luxury with its thick carpet in the rooms, Italian marble and travertine tile in the bathrooms, and it was ahead of its time in amenities offered to guests. Now, however, it is a place where vagrants fight over the rooms.

Blake Washington had once been a highly decorated war hero. That was before the alcohol and drugs took over. No matter what he does, he can't erase the horrors of the war from his head. Every time he closes his eyes, he sees the faces of those he killed for this country. The alcohol and drugs help him forget for a brief period. His ex-wife and family don't understand why he can't get on with life. Now, here he is, scavenging for a place to live every night, hitchhiking across America as much as possible and running from his past. Originally from Tennessee, he always wanted to see the deep south, so here he is. He has heard from a few people on the street that this is the best place to stay; no one seems to bother you at this old hotel. Blake even managed a great score today. Someone "misplaced" their phone in the john along with their wallet. The wallet had two hundred dollars in it, and he sold the cell phone on the street for another thirty. Blake was able to buy him some heroin and beer for later. He can forget about the ghosts that haunt him tonight.

Looking around, he can tell this used to be a great place to stay, but now mold and mildew cover the area. Blake doesn't care. It has been a while since he has slept in an actual bed, along with having four walls and a door to surround him. Once he becomes adjusted to the light, he opens what remains of the curtains and lets the moonlight filter into the room. Blake found some syringes on the floor of the main lobby and rinsed them out as best he could with a bottle of water he found on the street earlier today. All he can think about is the white powdery substance he purchased for a steal. The man selling it swore it was primo stuff.

Blake flicks the lighter with his thumb and holds the flame under the spoon he found in what he assumes was the dining room. He watches the white powder slowly dissolve. He fills the syringe with the warm liquid and anxiously waits for the pleasure that will soon consume his body. He ties his makeshift tourniquet on his arm and watches as the needle slides effortlessly into the vein. Several seconds later his cares fall away, the ghosts disappear and all that remains is a euphoria that he floats away on.

Blake's high is interrupted by another homeless person, "What the hell are you doing in here? This is my room!"

Blake is too high to care, "Sorry man I'll move on." Blake doesn't want a fight, besides there are plenty of rooms in this old hotel. Hell, he is so high right now he could sleep in the hall, it doesn't matter to him. All he wants is to ride this for as long as he can, but the man is still upset over Blake's presence.

****

The Regency is slated to be demolished later this week and the police have been asked to ensure the property is vacated. A task force has been set up to relocate the inhabitants to a shelter for now. When they enter the premises, they find two men fighting over a room. Before they can act, one of the men cuts open the other man's neck with a broken beer bottle. Blood gushes out from the open wound. Thinking quickly, an officer grabs a nearby piece of discarded material, possibly an old towel, and applies pressure. The ambulance is en route and should be here shortly. Officer Stapleton's partner is handcuffing the perpetrator so that he can be brought to the station. The remaining officers are rounding up the rest of the vagrants and transporting them to the shelter.

The medics keep the pressure applied to the wound and transport him to St. Anne's, since they are the closest hospital with a trauma unit. They radio the hospital to inform them about the incoming patient.

***

Nurse Jenkins pages me to advise me the patient should be here in two minutes. I had just dozed off after a long, tiring day. The on-call room is enveloped in blackness. Without bothering to turn on any lights, I fling the covers back and seek out my Crocs. As I am walking out the door I put on my white jacket, which has my name badge, and put the stethoscope around my neck.

There is an unusual amount of confusion surrounding the room. As I look around observing the mayhem, Nurse Jenkins chimes in, "We have a drunken patient who had his throat slashed with a broken beer bottle. By the look of his eyes, I suspect he may also be high. His pupils are dilated."

"Let's get a complete tox screen ordered then."

***

The man's blood is soaking through the multiple layers of gauze. Nurse Jenkins isn't sure which is worse, the trail of blood or the smell emanating from the man. She has a feeling it has been a long time since he has had any resemblance of a shower. The medic's gloved hand is pressed deeply into the gapping laceration in the patient's neck. The patient is making it difficult to tend to his wound. He is flailing about as the medics and orderlies try to move him to the gurney. They have to physically restrain him. One medic is covered in blood as he attempts to keep the agitated patient from harming himself further. The tape used to help the medic hold the towel and gauze in place is no longer sticking. Nurse Boudreaux administers a hefty dose of a sedative to the man so they can work on him.

Now that the patient is sedated he can be moved to the trauma gurney without further delay.

It is obvious that the combative patient is not only injured, but very much intoxicated. The stench emitting from the filthy, inebriated patient fills the small trauma room.

I notice all the blood, and instruct a nurse, "We need to cross match, and get me some O-negative blood here stat so a transfusion can be started."

Nurse Jenkins is on the phone with the lab stating, "We need five units of O-negative stat and send someone to do a cross match. You may need to call the local blood bank to see if they have any more O-negative just in case we can't get the patient cross-matched fast."

"I'll call them now and have someone down there with your blood."

Nurse Jenkins calls out to no one in particular, "Blood is on its way!"

The smell is becoming nauseating. "Is there any way we can have someone bathe him somewhat?"

Nurse Boudreaux has a scowl on her face, "I had a nurse trying already. This is better than when he first entered."

"It's going to be a very long surgery then." I am not looking forward to being trapped in a small OR room with the odor, but I need to get him into surgery stat.

Once the gauze is removed from the patient's neck, dark blood begins flowing out of the wound, using a gloved hand

I reach into the wound, find the source of the blood, and apply direct pressure. It isn't as bad as I originally thought, but I will need to repair the vein stat.

"As soon as we get a unit of O-negative blood started, let's move him to the OR."

All at once, a swarm of personnel is moving the patient into the operating room. My fingers never leave the inside of his neck. Once we reach the OR, I have an intern carefully swap places with me, so I can prep for surgery. In no time the patient is ready for me to repair the hemorrhage. With several swipes of my scalpel, I expose the entire jugular vein. The wound isn't bad enough to sacrifice the vein. With a few well-placed minuscule sutures, the hemorrhage is repaired.

While closing the gaping incision in his neck, I see an opportunity for yet another experiment. Acting quickly, I cut the patient's vocal cords.

I wonder how long it will take before someone realizes his vocal cords have been cut. With all the damage done to this man's neck, no one will suspect that I am responsible.

The stench from the patient seems to follow me throughout the hospital. After several minutes in the steaming hot shower, I can finally rid myself of the smell.

Chapter 17

George Hayworth has never been so embarrassed. What was he thinking anyway? Of all the people that this could happen to it had to be him. When he had searched for new forms of erotica he had never thought this would work. The blog posts he had found on the subject were too good for him to ignore. Curiosity got the best of him and he worked up the courage to try it.

The guy at the pet shop never even looked twice when he bought the gerbil. George had made up a story about surprising his daughter with it, and the man never asked. Just rang him up and handed him his new pet.

George thought he was cunning by going to different parts of the city to purchase everything he needed; not wanting anyone to see him walking from a hardware store to a pet store, and then to a sex toy shop.

When he got home, he arranged his goodies on the bed. He brought the pipe into the kitchen and washed it well with hot water and soap. The last thing he wanted was to use something unsanitary. It never even occurred to him that the gerbil was probably the most unsanitary thing he bought during the day.

At first it was an enjoyable experience, and then the damn thing started scratching. When George tried to pull the gerbil back out, the string he had tied to it broke. That is when all hell broke loose inside of his body. The pain was like nothing he had ever experienced. Driving himself to the emergency room was excruciating. The damn thing had stopped trying to claw its way out from inside George's body, but George felt as if his insides were on fire. Sitting was uncomfortable and his stomach was killing him. He had to undo the seatbelt while driving because even that was painful.

Somehow he has managed to crawl his way into the emergency room. The triage nurse asks him what his chief complaint is and he simply states a terrible stomach ache. He is not about to tell her he has a gerbil stuck in his ass.

After a few minutes she ushers him into an exam room. He crawls up on the exam table and curls into a fetal position. "Sir, I need you to sit up so that I can take your vitals."

He looks at her as if she is crazy, "Miss, there is no way I can sit up. It hurts way too bad."

The nurse can tell from his ashen face that he is in pain. "Let me get the doctor so we can get you something for the pain. I will also need to draw some blood for lab work."

He feels some stirring inside his stomach and realizes the gerbil must be making one more attempt to escape. He yowls in pain. "Damn it."

"Sir, where does it hurt?"

"My lower stomach."

When she tries to touch his stomach he holds up his hands defensively. "Please don't touch me."

***

The nurse can tell this will be a difficult patient. "I'll get the doctor."

When the emergency room doctor enters the room the patient is moaning uncontrollably. His eyes are puffy and red. "I'm Dr. Layton. What brings you to the emergency room tonight?"

The nurse has entered the room with the doctor, "Doc, can I please talk to you in private?"

Dr. Layton can't wait to hear this, "Nurse, please give us a minute? You can arrange for radiology to come get the patient."

"Yes doctor."

Turning back to his patient Dr. Layton asks, "So what seems to be the problem?"

****

In too much pain to worry about his dignity, he explains. "Well, Dr. Layton, I decided to try an erotica technique I found on the internet. The only problem is they didn't tell you what to do if the string broke on the damn thing. I've never been in so much pain in all my life. It hurts like hell to sit or even talk. "

Dr. Layton is afraid to even ask this next question, "What exactly did you try?"

"I went down to the pet store and bought a gerbil. You don't have to worry, I made sure the pipe was disinfected, but when I tried to pull the gerbil out, the damn string broke loose. The damn thing went crazy inside of me. My insides feel like they are on fire."

Dr. Layton tries to compose himself. "So let me make sure I understand you correctly. You have a live gerbil inside you?"

"Yes doctor. "

Dr. Layton has heard it all now. "We need to get you prepped for emergency surgery, but first I will need to get you to radiology to see where the gerbil is. When was the last time you felt it move?"

"It's been a few minutes."

"Okay, I need to do a rectal exam to see if I can feel it. If not, we will definitely need the x-rays."

Before beginning the rectal exam he reviews the patient's medical history. Nothing significant is noted. He checks his vitals once again. His abdomen is rigid. Even the slightest movement causes the man pain. Positive rebound. He listens to the patient's abdomen. There are no bowel sounds at all.

"Okay, Mr. Hayworth, I'm going to do the rectal now."

"I don't know doctor. I can't even move my legs."

"Let's see what we can get done, okay?"

Dr. Layton applies some Vaseline to his gloved index finger. The patient yells out in pain as he probes the rectum. There is blood around the anus and the deeper he probes, the more pain the patient complains of.

Dr. Layton steps out to the triage desk to see if the labs are back, and to find out if radiology is ready for the patient. The labs are back and the patient has an elevated white count.

A few minutes after radiology wheels the patient away, the x-ray technician calls down for Dr. Layton. "Dr. Layton, you will want to see this."

"Let me guess, you found a foreign object?"

"That's an affirmative."

"Now answer me this, is it moving?"

"Um, sir?"

"I need you to take several shots to see if it is moving, if at all possible?"

"Let me try, sir, and I'll let you know."

Dr. Layton suspects they are dealing with a perforated bowel. He calls Dr. Habersham, "Dr. Habersham, I hate to bother you, but I have an unusual case here that you may be interested in."

***

I really don't want to go perform surgery when there is another doctor on call, "Dr. Needham is on call."

"I realize that, but I also believe you may be the best doctor for this surgery. Dr. Needham is very good, but he is still young. I don't think he has ever handled an operation like this. Although, come to think of it, maybe you haven't ever seen this either."

"What's the case?"

"I have a thirty-eight year old man who presented to the emergency room with extreme abdominal discomfort. The patient admitted to me in private that he accidentally got a foreign object lodged in his rectum."

"Do I want to know what the object is?"

"Well, that is where the problem comes in. It was a gerbil sir. I'm waiting to see if radiology can ascertain if the gerbil is still alive, but there is a good bit of damage that I believe has been done to the bowel and surrounding area."

"I have worked on cases where vibrators had to be surgically removed, but a gerbil is a first. I am on my way in. I should be there in about fifteen minutes."

"I will try to have everything set up in OR for you sir."

Dr. Layton had helped prep other patients for trauma surgery with Dr. Habersham and knows how he likes things. Dr. Habersham may be this man's only chance. Nothing in medical school prepared Dr. Layton for anything like this. He has seen some strange things walk in through those emergency room doors, but this is a first. What amazes him is the things people will stick up their anus and vagina for a thrill. Over the years he has had to remove coke bottles, vegetables, and even a light bulb; but this is the first time he has heard of a gerbil. He wants to observe this surgery, but the emergency waiting room is already backing up.

Nurse Jenkins calls over to Dr. Layton, "Radiology is on the phone, sir."

"Dr. Layton here."

"It looks like your object is no longer moving sir. I have taken several films and it seems to be in the same place."

"Thank you. Please bring the patient and the films to OR. I will find out which room is free."

"Yes sir. Who will be doing the operation?"

"Dr. Habersham is on his way in."

Dr. Layton calls Nurse Boudreaux in, since she has worked with Dr. Habersham before, "Nurse Boudreaux, I know your shift doesn't start for a couple more hours, but Dr. Habersham is on his way in and I was wondering if you could assist him?"

"I can be there in a few minutes. What's the case?"

"We have a patient with a foreign object lodged where the sun doesn't shine, so to speak, and he needs immediate surgery."

"I'll be there shortly. I am already downtown."

Dr. Layton instructs one of the other on call nurses, "Let's get an IV started and put an NG tube down to empty his stomach, in case he had a meal earlier. Dr. Habersham is on his way to operate."

"Yes sir. Is the patient on his way back to the ER?"

"No, get up to the OR and prep him. We don't want to waste any time. When Dr. Habersham arrives he will want to begin the operation immediately."

***

I use a standard midline, exploratory laparotomy incision on George Hayworth. Since Mr. Hayworth isn't a small man, the incision stretches almost twelve inches down the midline, bypassing the belly button. I carefully feel around inside the abdomen until I find the culprit. The gerbil has passed away inside of Mr. Hayworth. The damage that the claws and teeth have done to the intestines is gruesome.

I have to run the bowel to make sure there are no more perforations. "Let's irrigate with antibiotics. I will need to do a colostomy in order to give the colon a chance to heal."

While I am repairing the damage to the bowel, I have missed a stitch. It will take a while before the seepage of the bowel contents causes any significant problems. There is a chance that the doctor who reverses the colostomy may discover my error, but I doubt it.

There is also significant damage done to the rectum, and for good measure I give his rectum a few extra stitches. This may alleviate the temptation to insert anything through this portal. It should be good and tight, although it may be painful for the patient to have a bowel movement for a while. No other lacerations are found. Even without my little alterations, the patient still has an uphill battle. He will be on antibiotics for a while to flush out his system.

Looking down at my work, I realize just how damn good I am. Now it is time to move on to the final stages of surgery. A cecostomy needs to be performed. A cecostomy is done so that cleansing enemas and antibiotics can be used to reduce the number of bacteria in the bowel. The procedure will also help decompress the large bowel and prevent distention until peristalsis is restored.

Penrose drains have been pulled out of incisions made in all four quadrants of the patient's stomach. Sterile safety pins are placed into each drain so they won't disappear back inside. The tubes are connected to a drainage bag. This will enable the nurse to irrigate the cecostomy tube with saline solution as necessary. Frequent dressing changes will also be needed, to keep the skin clean and dry.

Chapter 18

It has been three months since Drew Hornsby's motorcycle accident. The knee pain is unbearable at times. The cast has been off for about three weeks, and he still has to depend on crutches to walk. Even Dr. Cole has a hard time explaining his current problems and has suggested he might need another surgery. Drew is not looking forward to another surgery or hospital stay.

Dr. Cole performs the surgery the following Friday morning. The results are not what he was expecting. The tendon was cut in the accident, and not noticed by Dr. Habersham, or it was accidentally severed during the initial operation. Dr. Habersham's reputation is impeccable, so he doesn't believe a surgical mistake was made, but how did the man miss the torn tendon.

Now, to break the bad news to his patient, "Drew the surgery went well."

"Were you able to find out why I am still having problems walking?"

"Yes, I was, we found that the patellar tendon is torn. This tendon connects the bottom of the kneecap to the top part of the shin bone. It aids in the proper flexion and extension of the knee. Along with the other ligaments, tendons, muscles and bones of the knee joint, the patellar tendon supports the knee, and is essential in the proper movement of the joint. I repaired the tendon, but you may have permanent loss of motion, joint contractures, weakness and stiffness. I'm afraid this may be unavoidable."

"Is the torn tendon a result of the accident?"

"It's hard to say, but I am leaning that way."

"How was it missed in the first operation?"

"I haven't had a chance to talk to Dr. Habersham to see if he overlooked it, but don't you worry, I will sort this out. Unfortunately, you were rushed into surgery so fast that an MRI was never obtained beforehand, so I will have a hard time attributing it to the accident without Dr. Habersham's cooperation."

"But you are saying there is a good chance I can no longer do the same things I once was."

"I'm not saying that, but there is a good chance your knee will be nowhere near what it was before the accident. I have reviewed your previous medical records and find no complaint of knee problems before the accident."

"No, my knees were fine."

"Then it will be safe to say that this results from the accident. If your attorney needs me to put something in writing, please let me know. I really do feel for you, and I know this can't be easy at all."

"No, if only that driver would have been paying better attention."

"There is a chance after physical therapy, that the damage won't be too bad. It is one of those things that only time will tell."

"Thank you, doctor."

"It will be about six more weeks before we can start physical therapy, which will also delay the date when I can release you to go back to work."

"I understand. I was lucky; I purchased all the bells and whistles for insurance coverage. I'm not bringing in what I was before the accident, but at least it's enough to help us make ends meet."

"That's good. I've also instructed my billing clerk to hold off on billing you until the case is settled. Your attorney has been gathering all of my bills to show the insurance company. I also informed him we will wait until settlement to finalize any payments. Your medical insurance company has made their payments so we are good."

"Again, I can't thank you enough for that. My wife and I have been so worried about the medical bills piling up. Even the hospital has been good about accepting the insurance company's payment for now. I don't know what I would do if I had to pay my share right now."

"Don't worry about it. You concentrate on getting better. I will talk to the physical therapist and see if he can delay billing as well."

"Thanks again, doc. I seem to be thanking you a lot lately."

"No problem whatsoever."

Chapter 19

Jude Hudson is a local celebrity around Springport. He is a local boy that made it to an NFL pro football team. Before football season starts back up, he wants to see his Dad. While visiting though, he starts having the worst gas pains. At first he thinks it is from the fried foods he has indulged in while back home, but now he isn't so sure.

He can barely make it out of bed this morning, and his sister rushes him to St. Anne's to get checked out. "Doc, what is going on? This pain is killing me."

Dr. Alberts performs a preliminary exam on his patient. "Son, from what you are telling me, I suspect an acute gallbladder attack."

"What does that mean?"

"It could mean emergency surgery, but I won't know until we get an ultrasound done."

Jude Hudson hates hearing that he may have to undergo surgery. "Surgery? Practice is getting ready to start back up."

"Don't worry. Gallbladder surgery can be quick and relatively painless. You will be back to normal in no time. Let's not worry about surgery though until after we do the ultrasound."

A technician takes Jude to the ultrasound room. The radiologist confirms that it is an inflamed gallbladder.

"Mr. Hudson, you need to have your gallbladder removed immediately. It is quite inflamed and an infection has set in. Don't worry though; I have requested our top surgeon operate on you. You will be fine. The nurse is going to start you on some fluids and antibiotics to help fight the infection. You will be prepped for surgery and it will be over with before you know it."

"What is the recovery time?"

"In two weeks you will be as good as new and able to return to your normal activities."

Jude is still nervous about this surgery. This is the first time he has ever had a bad vibe about a doctor. Jude's sister, Amanda, walks into the room.

"What's wrong Jude, you look worried?"

"I don't know. Just nervous about this surgery I guess."

"There's nothing to worry about. The doctor said it's a simple procedure. Besides, I did some asking around and you have a top notch surgeon. From what I gather, he has a great pair of hands, just like you."

"I know. I just can't explain this feeling I am having."

***

Amanda knows her brother is overreacting. These doctors will take good care of him. No one wants to be the one that did anything to hurt Jude Hudson. Football fans everywhere love her brother. Even the media loves Jude, with his famous grin and mesmerizing eyes. Jude isn't like a lot of the other famous football players either. He is easy going, with a great sense of humor. She has to admit that Jude is an all-around decent person. If something were to happen to him during surgery, millions of fans would boycott the hospital. She is sure no one would want that.

***

I am finishing some paperwork before ending my shift when I hear the page to call the ER. "Dr. Habersham, I know you are getting ready to leave, but Dr. Alberts has a patient in the ER that needs emergency gall bladder surgery and he was wondering if you could perform the surgery."

Gallbladder surgery can be done rather quickly by laparoscopy and shouldn't take up too much of my time. Besides, this may give me the perfect opportunity to test out a new experiment. If all goes well, I may be able to nick a bile duct during surgery. "Tell Dr. Alberts I can perform the surgery. Let's get the patient up to OR 3, it is available."

"I'll let Dr. Alberts know."

I head to the OR to prepare for surgery. If a bile duct is cut during surgery, the bile will leak into the abdominal area and cause an infection. With the patient already on antibiotics, the nurses may not even notice another infection. Sometimes it is even months before a patient knows there is a possible complication from the surgery.

Chapter 20

Tyler Landry isn't ready to die. It isn't hunting season, but he thought it would be fun to take a few practice shots before the season opens. He wants to make sure his stand is ready. He turned 50 this year and never thought about dying before today. His doctor warned him over the last couple of years to keep his diabetes under better control. Tyler had figured he would just grab a quick cup of coffee this morning before heading out, anxious to leave. He wasn't planning on being out here long, so he was planning to eat when he got home. He should have never climbed that stand. Thank God his wife became worried when he didn't answer his phone. Unfortunately, he fell four hours before she found him.

The paramedics rushed him to St. Anne's Hospital where he is waiting to have emergency surgery to stop the internal bleeding. The nurse is preparing his IV and then he will be off to the operating room. His lungs are filling with fluid, making it difficult to breath.

"Nurse, give it to me straight. Am I going to die?"

Nurse Boudreaux looks at him in sympathy, "Not if Dr. Habersham has anything to say about it. He has a high success rate, and refuses to let his patients die on the operating table."

All Tyler can think about is the excruciating pain that penetrates his body with every attempt to breathe. He can hear the liquid in his lungs gurgling. "Can I please have another blanket? It is so blasted cold in here."

***

Nurse Boudreaux tries to make him a little more comfortable. That is all she can do for now. His color is looking poor; he is turning a grayish color. He does indeed feel clammy, which is never a good sign. She feels his neck to check on his pulse. It is faint. They are getting ready to move him into the OR where he will be put under anesthesia. They will need to hurry if Dr. Habersham has any chance of saving him. The patient's breathing is getting weaker, and the gurgling louder. A chest tube has been put in to help drain the fluid in his lungs, but the fluid is building up faster than the tubes are draining it.

***

The floor is busier than usual this morning. Several private physicians have minor procedures scheduled for today, along with the usual emergency operations. I, for one, despise when I have to wait for an available OR, and I inform Nurse Boudreaux to have a doctor push back his elective procedure. My case takes precedence! It is a matter of life or death. Clearly this is going to be one of those days that surgery is once again overbooked.

The patient is intubated and anesthetized. I am waiting on the scalpel from the nurse. The anesthesiologist is guarding the head of the table. Several nurses bustle about the room. An electrocardiogram, EKG for short, monitors the patient's heart rhythms.

The OR is quiet except for the steady sounds of the monitors and machines. No one speaks as I operate. The anesthesiologist breaks the silence, "Blood pressure is dropping."

I don't like hearing that there are problems with anesthesia while I am operating. "What's going on? Is the patient stable?" If you can't tell by now, I am getting extremely impatient.

"You're good to go. Blood pressure is stabilizing."

I use the retractor to peer deeper into the wound. "Suction!" There is still too much blood to get a good view of the wound.

After the operation is complete I give further instructions, "Let's get this patient up to ICU. Don't bother me unless we have another operation." I may sound crass but I've done my part. The patient has been saved. Now I have to wait for the next patient that needs their life saved. For the last several years this was my life, a top notch trauma surgeon. Whatever the case, all the patients have the same problem; they need a miracle to save their lives. By the time I get to them, triage has been completed and the patient has been prepped for surgery. Unlike my fellow colleagues, I never worry about whether my patient is going to live or die. I never worry about failure, I am that good.

Chapter 21

Several weeks have passed since Kirstin Hebert had spoken with her brother Bill about the possibility of talking to a medical malpractice attorney. Kirstin has been tossing and turning, worrying about her financial situation. The more she thinks about it, the more depressed she becomes. The depression isn't helping matters.

Kirstin has finally made up her mind, "Bill, it's me. I've decided to take your advice. Did you ever get the name of a medical malpractice attorney?"

Kirstin knows this may be her only hope. The bills are mounting up and there is no income coming in. The hospital bills are more than she expected.

"I did get the name of a top notch attorney from my boss. He said that you should call Gregory Chaisson. From what I understand, there is no charge unless he wins. He will probably be able to tell you immediately if you have a case or not."

"Thank you Bill. Will you be able to come with me?"

"Just let me know when you have a meeting with him and I will be there. I don't see a problem with me getting a little time off."

"I don't know what I would do without you and mom right now. You've been my lifesavers."

"That's what family is for Sis."

Attorney Gregory Chaisson is able to meet with Kirstin the next day. Mr. Chaisson is in his early forty's, with a full head of dark brown hair that is starting to show some gray. He has an air of competence about him that helps put Kirstin at ease. Kirstin was afraid he will be a stuffy old attorney, but he is anything but. He leads her and Bill into a large office. One wall is lined floor to ceiling with bookshelves overflowing with books. A large window overlooks the riverside. The office smells of wealth. Kirstin sure hopes Bill is correct and he doesn't charge unless he wins. There is no way she can afford him otherwise.

Chaisson listens carefully to what Kirstin has to tell him. She is surprised at his knowledge of the medical terminology. She is actually grateful someone understands it. It went right over her head when the doctor was explaining it to her.

"Mrs. Hebert, how much did your husband bring home a year?"

"Without overtime, it was $36,000, roughly. But he had been putting in extra hours and his paychecks were almost doubled. That night was the first night he didn't work late, and he had stopped off at the bar to have a beer with his buddies."

"Do you know if the bartender tried to stop him from driving, or cut him off after he had a few?"

"No, I don't. I never talked to anyone from there after the accident. I believe they sent flowers to the funeral home."

"We might have a case against them also. We can hold them liable for serving him after he was over his limit and then letting him drive drunk."

"I don't know about that. Dale was an adult and it was his decision and his decision alone."

"True, but I just won a case where a family was hit by a drunk driver, and the bartender failed to cut him off and take away his keys. The judgment was a nice amount. This might work out in your favor. The bar may settle quicker than the hospital, and that would get some money into your pocket sooner."

"I thought you handled medical malpractice cases?"

"I do, but on occasion I handle personal injury and wrongful death cases. I can afford to be picky about what cases I take. Now, how old was your husband?"

"Thirty-eight."

"So, if we take into account that he would have worked until the age of sixty-five, that gives us twenty-seven years for loss of income. Not taking into consideration cost of living increases and whatever raises he may have been awarded, that would give you approximately $972,000 in loss of income. I will need to hire someone to work up the accurate figures to include medical insurance and the like, but at a minimum, I wouldn't settle for less than $2 million dollars for loss of income and such; plus we need to take into account pain and suffering and loss of consortium. This case is indeed worth the effort that I can put into it. I will have my secretary bring you in the releases that I need signed in order to obtain the medical records, employment records and anything else I may need to help the case."

"That's it, then?"

"That's it. The hospital will probably be slow at responding to the request, but you never know. I have a feeling they have already notified their insurance carrier, so it may move along faster than expected. My contingency fee is thirty-three percent plus expenses. I usually try to work that figure into the settlement amount. If anyone calls you to discuss the case, please do not speak with them. You can refer all such calls to my office. Someone here will address them."

"Thank you so much. I really do dread having to sue, but I didn't know what else to do."

"Think of it this way, your husband didn't expect to go into the hospital, contract MRSA and die either, did he?"

"No, I suppose he didn't."

***

Gregory Chaisson is confident that in front of a jury he can create enough sympathy for the widow and her children to get a substantial judgment, not only from the hospital but the bar as well. This is a slam-dunk case. There is also a chance that the insurance companies will want to settle before the case even gets off the ground. He has a feeling that the hospital will want to sweep this under the rug as fast as possible. The hospital is his best bet because they have deeper pockets.

"Mrs. Hebert, there is one thing I can promise you, we may never know exactly how your husband contracted MRSA, but there is no way it happened anywhere but in the hospital. The hospital is going to have to pay, and they will pay big."

***

It's not collecting a substantial amount of money that Kirstin Hebert is worried about, but she wants to make sure it is enough to help her and her children get by. She is ready to put this behind them and start a new life. "How soon do you expect a settlement offer to be made?"

"That's hard to pinpoint, but I say in the next few weeks. I doubt it will take more than a couple of months for this matter to be closed."

"That soon?"

"It's hard to deny the cold hard facts of the case. I don't see where the insurance company will want to have this case hanging over them. I look for them to make an offer quickly, to get this matter behind them. I can't guarantee an amount, but I would expect it to be a substantial figure."

"Mr. Chaisson, thank you for all your help in this matter. I don't know what I would have done without you."

"Mrs. Hebert, it is my pleasure. As soon as I hear from the insurance company I will call you."

When they are back in the car, Kirstin looks over at Bill. "Bill, I want to thank you for pushing me into doing this. Without your help and support I would never have even considered this. This whole experience has been awful, but at least now maybe I can stop worrying about how I will survive financially. I don't know what the kids or I would do without you and mom."

Bill reaches over and squeezes her hand, "You don't owe me a thing. I'm just glad things may be working out for you."

Chapter 22

At 4:30 Friday afternoon, Nurse Boudreaux calls to ask me to come in. A four year old girl, Jasmine Breaux, has been mauled by an Akita. That is a big dog, and I can only imagine the damage that has been done to her body. The attending ER doctor is stitching up the wounds he can, but there is serious internal damage.

This little girl can be the next experiment. Now, what possible body part can I remove from her?

Decisions, decisions, decisions. I'm thinking the little girl will have part of her liver removed. She will still have a good portion of her liver remaining. If for some unknown reason she needs it later on, it won't be of any consequence to me.

The parents, Daniel and Angel Breaux, are busy pacing the waiting room floor praying that everything will be okay. Jasmine had just gotten home from school and wanted to play out front for a little while. She had some new sidewalk chalk she wanted to try out. She told her mom that she was going to write a special message for her daddy to see when he came home from work. Angel was on the front porch talking to a neighbor when she saw the dog come charging into the yard. Before she knew what was happening, he had a hold of Jasmine and didn't want to let go. Thankfully, her neighbor knew enough to grab the water hose and start spraying the animal. Another neighbor heard the commotion and grabbed his gun. It didn't take long for the paramedics to get to the scene and have her on her way to the hospital.

From my first observations of the little girl, it appears as though the dog picked her up by her stomach and shook her like a rag doll. I am not a compassionate person by any means, but I would have shot the dog. What on earth could have provoked it to cause so much damage to this little girl? For a moment, I contemplate not doing further research on her, but that is only for a fleeting moment.

Nurses are busy preparing the OR for surgery. Currently the bleeding seems to be under control. The internal damage may not be as bad as first feared, but her life is still in danger. Everyone in the OR knows the gravity of the situation. The only sounds emitted in the room are quiet and controlled. I can hear the rhythmic hissing of the ventilator, the beeps of the monitors and the faint click of metal on metal from the surgical instruments.

"Suction." The nurse follows my instructions without question. More blood joins the considerable amount already in the suction container.

"More suction, there's still bleeding present." I look for the various puncture wounds causing the bleeding.

I apply even more internal sutures while a nurse dabs the sweat off of my forehead. As I call for an instrument with my right hand up, the instrument is immediately slapped into my hand. We are working in such unison today that we rarely miss a beat, like a well-orchestrated dance.

Chapter 23

Irene Metz wakes up slowly this morning. Her daughter and grandkids are coming to visit her today. She is ecstatic. It has been a while since their last visit.

She is stiff this morning from arthritis. Whenever her joints are stiff and painful it usually means rain; old age has turned her into a walking barometer. She is only sixty-two, but today she feels as if she is eighty. She looks at herself in the mirror before heading downstairs; she is starting to show her age. At one time she always made sure her hair was colored, never allowing gray hair to show. Now her hair is gray and straggly. It is a rat's nest this morning, and will take some time to fix before her company arrives. She also notices a few more wrinkles. She misses her smooth face and slim body. This person looking back at her is a stranger. Her husband has been dead for two years now, and she has stopped caring about her appearance. That needs to change. She is still young and needs to get out more, stop being a recluse and waiting for the grandkids to come visit her. There is no reason she can't go visit them.

As Irene walks downstairs, she feels herself falling and tries to grab on to something, anything. Her first thought is that her daughter has been begging her to move downstairs in order to avoid the stairs, but she was too stubborn to listen. She is clawing wildly at the air, hoping to find something to stop her fall. She sees the banister and tries to grab it, but it is just out of her reach. She closes her eyes, anticipating the pain that is to about come from the fall. Her shoulder hits the stairs right before her head does.

"Ugh!" she cries out. Her shoulder is throbbing in pain and her head feels like it is splitting. She is having great difficulty trying to stand. She can see and feel the warm blood flowing down her face from the head wound, but she knows head wounds always tend to bleed a lot. She tries to crawl towards the phone, but it is taking more energy than she has right now. She needs to rest a little while before trying again. Her surroundings are starting to sway and spin violently. She is too disoriented to move.

She pushes through the nausea and pain. She doesn't want her daughter and grandkids to find her like this. That is her motivation to push on. It takes her a while to reach the phone. She manages to dial 911. Hopefully they arrive before her company.

By the time the EMT's arrive at the house, she is having slurred speech and they are concerned about swelling of the brain. She overhears one of them saying something about surgery to relieve pressure. The EMT's hook her up to monitors and IV's before leaving the house with her. Twenty minutes later, she is being wheeled into the emergency room at St. Anne Hospital.

She is in the operating room before she knows it. The atmosphere in here is too cold and impersonal for her. She wishes now she had asked them to call her daughter. The bright lights are hurting her eyes. Nurses are moving quickly around her preparing for the emergency surgery. Irene feels so helpless, strapped to the operating table waiting for the anesthesiologist.

***

The fall has caused a bleed in her head. Blood is slowly leaking into the delicate tissues of her brain. The blood collects in the space between the "dura mater" and the skull. The bleeding is causing a hematoma that presses on the brain, causing a rapid increase of the pressure inside the head. I have been called in to perform surgery to prevent additional brain injury. There may be a rapid worsening within minutes or hours, from drowsiness to coma and death, so time is of the essence. If the neurosurgeon hadn't been tied up in another surgery, then I would never have been given this opportunity. It is fate.

This is the kind of emergency surgery I've been waiting for. It is imperative to reduce pressure within the brain. To do this I will have to drill a small hole in the skull to relieve pressure and allow drainage of the blood from the brain. This may give me the perfect opportunity to experiment with a lobotomy. I never thought I would actually get a chance to try this experiment.

This procedure will be a "blind" lobotomy, as I will not know the exact path of the small wire knife. The instrument I plan on using has an open steel loop at its end; when closed, the loop severs the tissue within it. It will have to be done quickly to not be noticed. Over the years, I have learned how to use my tools of choice while they are tucked into the sleeves of my gown. So far these actions have gone unnoticed. Once the hole has been drilled, I plan on inserting the wire and cutting out a sample of brain tissue. The outcome cannot be determined, so the operation may produce mixed results. There may be a difference in behavior or there may be no noticeable difference. And the best part is that any results of this little experiment will be blamed on the head injury. No one will ever know that a partial lobotomy has been performed.

Once the patient's condition had been analyzed, I seem almost to go into a robotic mode. I instruct Nurse Boudreaux, "I need you to shave her head so that I can drill the burr holes."

"Yes doctor." Nurse Boudreaux informs the patient, "I will have to shave your hair ma'am, but don't worry, it grows back fast." The patient's gray hair is caked with blood from the laceration at the scalp line. Once the area has been shaved, she applies Betadine solution to the area.

I work silently; concentrating on the procedure at hand. The burr holes have to be made with exact precision. The OR nurses are accustomed to my style and temper. They always do their best to anticipate my needs before I raise my voice. My surgical assistant is standing by in case I need a hand, which I won't. Everything is going smoothly.

***

Irene's daughter, Nicole, has been by her side since she found out her mother was in the hospital. She has felt so guilty for not visiting her as often as she should. Letting life get in the way is no excuse for not visiting her mother more than every now and then. In the blink of an eye, Nicole could have lost her, and then what would she have done.

Irene is finally waking up after the surgery. The neurosurgeon arrived after the trauma surgeon managed to relieve the pressure inside her head. Nicole is grateful to both.

"Mom, I love you so much. I'm so glad you are okay."
Nicole doesn't know why she is saying this. The
neurosurgeon has warned her he won't know the extent of
damage until her mom is awake and he can give her a
proper exam. From the preliminary tests, it looks like she
will be just fine and Nicole is praying that there is nothing
wrong.

"Duhhh...."

"Mom, I'm sorry I can't understand you. Take it easy."

"Mmmahhh...."

The nurse enters the room as Irene is speaking, "Oh good, I
see you are awake. How are we feeling today?"

"Wahhhhh....."

"I'm sorry ma'am, do you want water?"

Irene shakes her head no, "Wahhh...."

The nurse checks Irene's vitals and returns to the nurses'
station to place a call to Dr. Alden. "Dr. Alden, Irene Metz is
awake and trying to talk. You might want to get down here.
I think there may be more neurological damage than you
expected."

"I'm on my way. Is her daughter still there?"

"Yes sir, she is in the room."

The nurse walks back into the patient's room, "Mrs. Davis,
Dr. Alden is on his way in. He is going to examine your

mother now that she is awake and explain a few more things to you."

"Thank you. I'll wait for him before I head home then."

Nicole holds her mom's hand, "Don't worry Mom, it's going to be all right."

When Dr. Alden arrives, he does a cursory exam. "It looks like the area of the brain that was damaged in the fall is the area responsible for speech, Mrs. Davis. Your mom is able to retain the ability to understand what we are saying to her, but she is unable to articulate coherent speech herself. This may be a permanent problem, or when the swelling goes down, it may resolve itself. It also looks like she may have a minimum amount of paralysis on her right side as a result of the fall."

"What about her quality of life? Is she going to be dependent on others, or will she be able to live on her on?"

"It's still too early to tell, but I'm sorry to say that with your mom's age, that some of the symptoms may be permanent. Her insurance coverage will only allow her a short stay here at the hospital, and after that, we will be forced to move her to a rehabilitation center for further follow up."

"I don't understand. The insurance company is going to force you to move her to a nursing home."

"I'm sorry, but that is the way the system works. We are only allowed to keep patients here for a short time before we have to discharge them or move them into a rehabilitation center."

"Mom has always been very independent. I don't see her approving of this."

"Unfortunately, the insurance company doesn't ask the patient if it is something they want or not, it is mandatory. Depending on the extent of care she needs, you may want to consider moving her into your house for a period of time to help care for her, especially if this is something that may make her more comfortable. I do have to warn you though; this can present its own challenges. Your mom will get frustrated that she can't articulate what she wants to say and may act out."

"Yes, of course. I plan on doing whatever I can to help mom recuperate."

"As much as people hate putting their loved one in a rehabilitation facility, please understand that sometimes it is for the best. The staff there is trained to care for the patient. Sometimes this helps the recovery process move along at a better pace. The therapists there can help with speech and whatever physical limitations there may be."

"I will keep that in mind. Thank you again, Dr. Alden."

***

Dr. Alden goes back to his office and reviews Irene Metz's hospital and surgical charts one more time. What is he missing? The injuries Irene suffered from the fall were extensive, but he doesn't see anything that would cause the problems she is having. While she is still here at the hospital, he will order another MRI to check her brain.

Maybe there is a bleed that was missed, but he doesn't think so.

When he gets the next MRI's findings, he is stunned. There has to be a mistake. There is still a significant amount of swelling in the area, but if the image is correct, the MRI also shows that a small portion of the brain matter is missing. That isn't possible though. Could it be that Dr. Habersham accidentally went too far with the drill? But if that was the case, there would be more damage. Dr. Alden will need to review Irene Metz's previous medical records to see if maybe she had a previous brain injury or surgery.

The following morning Irene Metz's daughter is anxious to see if there has been any improvement in her mother's health. Dr. Alden is already in her room. "There is very little improvement this morning. The MRI does not show any evidence of bleeding. However, I do need to know if your mother ever mentioned a brain injury or surgery at some point in her life?"

"No, I don't recall. I take it the MRI showed something?"

Dr. Alden will have to answer this question carefully. "The MRI is inconclusive. There is some swelling in the area and I will repeat the test in a few days. A small injury did appear on the image, but it could be nothing. It is not consistent with her injury. At this time, your mother still does not have use of her right side and her speech is still affected."

***

Nicole sees that her mom is waking up and walks over and kisses her on the forehead. "Good morning mom. You seem to have a little more color in your cheeks today. Dr. Alden is here, and we are discussing your progress so far."

Dr. Alden turns to his patient, "We are going to give you a few more days of rest and then we will need to start physical and speech therapy. Now, I don't want to alarm you, but the insurance company has instructed us that they believe you will benefit from a rehabilitation center better than staying here at the hospital. They will be able to address your needs better." This is the part Dr. Alden hates. No one wants to hear that they will basically be moved to a nursing home.

Irene Metz is shaking her head vigorously. Nicole hates this. "Don't worry mom, it's going to be alright. In no time you will be back to your normal self, just wait and see. The rehabilitation center won't be permanent. If nothing else, you can move in with us. This is going to work out just fine." Now if only Nicole can make herself believe that statement she will feel better about this whole situation.

Chapter 24

Abigail Verdun, Mary Kate Broussard, Leah Sellers and Susan Perry have been inseparable friends since grade school. When Leah mentions that her brothers are going to be away for the weekend, it is mutually agreed that they should take their four wheelers for a ride. Leah's brothers refuse to let them use the four wheelers. None of the girls are familiar with four wheelers, and how difficult and dangerous can it be.

Leah Sellers lives on a massive plantation, with plenty of land to go riding on. The sugarcane has just been harvested so they can go riding over there. That will give them plenty of open land to practice on. The plantation has been in Leah's family for generations, and their money has been made from sugar cane. Her dad loves to remind her that not only is sugarcane an integral part of the south Louisiana economy and culture, but her family's as well.

As soon as school lets out, they met at Leah's house. Donning jeans, t-shirts and tennis shoes, the girls head out to the barn where the four wheelers are kept. Leah has managed to sneak into her brothers' room and get the keys. Her parents are both gone, so there is no way they can get in trouble.

Mary Kate is a little nervous about riding, but she doesn't want to sound like a big baby, "What about helmets? Do we need to wear them?"

"I'm not sure where my brothers keep the helmets, but it's not like we are going to be racing or anything, we will be fine. "

Mary Kate is still worried, "I have no idea how to drive this thing."

Abigail can't wait, "I'll drive, and you can ride with me."

Leah isn't about to miss the chance of driving, "I'm driving, too. Susan, it looks like you are stuck with me."

Susan doesn't care. She doesn't see what the big deal is, but she doesn't want to be left out in case they end up having fun.

The accident happens so fast it catches the girls by complete surprise. Leah is having so much fun on the small gravel road running along the back of the cane field that she never hears Abigail coming. Abigail is going faster than she realizes, loses control in the curve, and plows into the four wheeler driven by Leah. When the two four wheelers collide Mary Kate is pinned in between the machines and the other girls are thrown off. Susan is able to get to her cell phone out of her pocket and calls her dad and then 911.

"We had a four wheeler accident on the Sellers property, dad. Mary Kate looks to be hurt pretty bad. I'm not sure about the rest of us. I may have broken my leg, it hurts really bad!"

Susan's dad calls the rest of the parents as he drives out to the Sellers house. What on earth possessed these girls to go four-wheeler riding of all things?

Mary Kate has to be airlifted to St. Anne's Hospital in Springport after she is freed from between the four wheelers. The other three girls are transported there via ambulance, since their injuries don't seem to be life threatening. None of the medics at the scene believe Mary Kate will survive the twenty minute ambulance ride. Her chances are slightly improved with the short helicopter ride. Mary Kate has suffered a concussion, internal injuries, possible broken bones and a mangled leg.

***

I am getting ready to head home when I hear the call come into the Emergency Room. A trauma patient is being airlifted to the hospital, and ETA is two minutes. The remaining accident victims will arrive via ambulance shortly. She was involved in a very serious four wheeler accident and is in and out of consciousness. I inform Nurse Boudreaux to get the OR ready stat.

Nurse Jenkins is the duty nurse tonight. I give her further instructions. "There is no time to waste! As soon as the young girl lands, I want a team out there. Bring her directly into the OR. We can suture her in there, but with the internal injuries, it is best to be in a place where we are more likely to save the girl's life."

The medic has informed the hospital that none of the young girls were wearing helmets. I leave orders for when the other three girls arrive to have CT scans and x-rays done. Why were these young girls riding without any type of head protection?

I hear Nurse Jenkins calling me, "Dr. Habersham, the medic called to say he believes one of the other girls may have a broken jaw."

"I will start work on the young girl that is being airlifted in. See if you can call Dr. Williams in to take care of the one with the possible broken jaw."

"Yes sir."

I meet the helicopter so that I can get a firsthand look at what I am getting ready to operate on. The girl can't be more than sixteen years old. I will need to do a quick assessment of her injuries. The medics help get her in the OR. We carefully lift her off of the hardboard stretcher and onto the operating table. The nurses quickly prep her. Nurse Boudreaux is barking orders out, "Let's get her vitals and an IV started. I need someone to cut her clothes off of her."

I have a few orders of my own, "Let's draw a blood sample and run a panel, STAT."

One of the younger nurses starts cutting off her clothes. The denim jeans on her mangled legs is making it difficult to remove her clothing. Her jeans and shirt ended up basically being shredded in order to not jostle the patient too much. The young girl gives the nurse a horrified look as she is cutting off her clothes. Unfortunately, modesty and dignity can't become an issue when trying to save someone's life.

"I'm sorry honey, but this is something that I need to do. Don't worry, we will cover you with a sheet as soon as we can." Another nurse steps in to help pull away her clothing and cover her. The young girl is laying on the gurney, taking quick rapid breaths. Her eyes sweep the room. There are smears of blood running down her body from various scrapes and cuts.

Her mangled leg is bent at an awkward angle. The emergency room doctor is busy helping the nurses get the young girl ready for surgery. Her leg will need to be placed in a splint until it can be repaired. The internal bleeding has to be resolved before the leg can be worked on. Looking down at her, he states, "This is going to hurt some, but we need to get your leg splinted." As the bone is straightened, it makes a loud crunch, we can hear the bones grinding as the leg is put back into its original position. The girl is now pale from the pain. She lets out a sharp shriek from the agonizing pain. "I am so sorry, but the worst part is over with." He has her leg splinted in record time.

Nurse Boudreaux says, "Dr. Habersham, her blood pressure is 90 over 60 and her pulse is 110."

I don't like that her pulse is rapid and her blood pressure is low. She is losing blood from somewhere, and we need to find out where, now. "Let's hurry up, I need to get started. She is bleeding internally."

The young girl is opening and closing her eyes nervously. Nurse Boudreaux tries to calm her. "You need to stay still a little longer sweetheart. You are in the hospital. The doctor is going to make you all better."

She nods her head.

The x-ray machine is wheeled into the OR to get images of her neck and head, but I suspect she has a mild concussion. She may have been lucky, in that she was pinned between the two four-wheelers. Her main injuries are the mangled legs, which will need a massive amount of staples, sutures and hardware. Her blood pressure and heart rate have me worried though. "I'm going to check over your body really quick to see if there are any injuries other than your legs."

Again, she nods that she understands. "I'm going to press on your stomach; if it hurts anywhere you let me know?"

She nods her head, then gasps, "I hurt so bad!"

"I know it hurts. As soon as we can, I'm going to have the nurse give you a shot to help with the pain."

When I press on her left side, she squeals out in pain.

By the time I am done with the quick physical exam, the x-rays are ready for review. Nurse Boudreaux administers the pain medicine into the IV. "You are doing great, sweetheart. It won't be long now before you feel better. Hang in there."

"X-rays look clear, but her blood pressure is too low." Nurse Boudreaux announces.

I know she is bleeding internally, "Quick, prepare her for a wash." A "wash" is when a saline solution is injected into the membrane of the abdominal cavity and then aspirated back into the syringe. If the saline solution comes back bloody, then blood is present where it shouldn't be. "It's definitely bloody. I think she has a ruptured spleen. Let's go! I will start on her abdomen, someone pack the leg with gauze to control the bleeding. I will work on it later."

Nurse Boudreaux is already working on applying dressings to the girl's legs, "Yes sir." She turns to the patient, "You're doing great. The doctor is going to take a look and see what is going on inside of you and then he will fix that leg of yours."

She nods yes, but her eyes are filled with tears.

I further instruct Nurse Boudreaux, "You may have to put a tourniquet on her leg to help control the bleeding, but we should be okay. Have we heard from her parents yet?"

"They are in the waiting room. They already signed the consent forms. They just want you to save their daughter." That is all I need to know. The hospital requires parental consent unless it is an emergency. Even though this is a true emergency, it always helps to make sure all bases are covered. I certainly don't want a medical malpractice suit filed against me.

The assisting surgeon states, "I can work on the leg if you'd like."

I can't believe the gall of him even suggesting that, "That won't be necessary. I may need you to help with the internal injuries. We want to get her patched up as fast as possible."

"Yes doctor."

The young girl's insides are a mess, but after the blood is suctioned out, I am able to find where the bleeding is coming from. The spleen has a small tear. A quick couple of sutures, and I fix that right up. I close up and move on to her leg.

While I have been working on her internal injuries, the x-ray tech has taken several films of her leg to identify the broken bones. As I unpack the gauze from her leg, I see the Achilles tendon perfectly. In one quick movement, I cut it without anyone noticing. I just can't help this little experiment, besides it's the young girl's own fault. If she hadn't been riding the four-wheeler, this would never have happened.

I wonder what will result from the cut Achilles's tendon. I know she might be able to walk, but not well. It is imperative that a cut Achilles' be repaired as soon as possible; otherwise, the cut ends retract and deteriorate, making the repair extremely complicated or impossible. Either way, I don't know and don't care, it's just an experiment. The outcome will depend on how fast her doctor finds the damage. X-rays prior to the operation will show the Achilles' tendon is fine, so they doctor will be left wondering how she ended up with such a cut. I doubt they will ever put it together. I do know that it will be a while before it's noticed, because of the leg fracture. It will be weeks before the cast is removed.

After the surgery, Larry Stevens catches me as I am walking down the hall. "You will go talk to the girls' parents. They have a lot of influence in this town and deserve to hear about their daughter's prognosis from you, and not the nurse or assistant surgeon."

I glare at him. I despise talking to parents, especially ones that would let their teenage daughter ride a four wheeler without a helmet. She is lucky that she doesn't have a brain injury. I also know better than to push my luck too far with Larry Stevens. If he were to inform the Board of Directors that I pissed off an affluent couple who donate money to the hospital, then my job could be on the line. Guess I will have to play nice this time.

Initial impressions are always important. I can normally read people right away. I can tell these parents pay more attention to their looks than anything else, especially the mother. I suspect she has her plastic surgeon on speed dial. Botox is probably her best friend and there is no way those boobs are real. She is going to regret that decision when she gets older and her back starts giving her problems.

The dad has a laid back look about him. He probably spends most of his time in the tanning bed. From his bone structure, I'm betting he was a jock in high school. He is very alert, though.

"Mr. and Mrs. Broussard, my name is Dr. Habersham. I operated on your daughter. When she was brought into the hospital, it was suspected she had internal injuries in addition to the damage done to her legs. The legs have multiple lacerations and were placed in splints instead of casts, to allow the dressings on her wounds to be changed. Her spleen was also damaged, and that was repaired."

The dad absorbs everything that I have said and ask, "So you did not have to remove the spleen?"

"No, we did not have to do a splenectomy. The operation went smoothly, very uneventful really. She is in recovery and doing well."

"Can we see her now?"

"No problem. I must warn you though; she does have an IV in her arm and a tube in her nose. There are also wires on her upper chest monitoring her vital signs. This is all standard medical procedure after a surgery. Don't let it worry you."

The mother is extremely grateful. "Thank you so much Dr. Habersham. She is our baby girl, and I don't know what I would do if something had happened to her."

I quickly leave the room before I say something damaging. I wonder what the parents will think when they find out their daughter may have suffered permanent damage to her ankle. This serves them right for being so irresponsible. The parents should never have bought a four wheeler for the girl, and they should have taught her not to be so careless while riding it. In all honesty, this is really all the girl's fault. If she had never come into my operating room, then I would have never been given the chance to experiment on her.

Chapter 25

Several years ago the hospital added a coffee shop.
Business has been booming since it opened. Doctors and
patients alike stop by and order coffee, latte, espresso or
cappuccinos before heading to their destination. I order my
usual amaretto latte before heading to the OR.

The corridors of St. Anne's Hospital are busy. They are
always busy at this time of the day though. Nurse
Boudreaux catches me as I am heading towards the OR. She
wants to let me know about our next patient. I have
already rinsed my mouth, and was hoping the coffee would
help mask the smell, but you can still smell the alcohol on
my breath. Whoever said vodka doesn't have a smell never
drank a fifth right before an operation. I can see the disdain
on her face. Yes, I admit I have been drinking, but
occasionally, even I have to relieve some stress. Besides, I
can do these operations with my eyes closed and one hand
tied behind my back. Besides, I'm not worried about Nurse
Boudreaux, she knows better than to confront me about my
drinking.

Samuel Bellue is waiting to be operated on. This morning,
he woke up with shoulder and abdominal pain. The ER
doctor suspects possible internal bleeding. The patient's
abdomen is full of blood.

The operating room staff is busy preparing Mr. Bellue for his
surgery. Once I am through scrubbing, a nurse helps to
dress me in a sterile mask, gown and gloves. Nurse
Boudreaux still has not confronted me about the smell of

alcohol on my breath, but as we are scrubbing in, she keeps watching my movements. I guess it's time to bring Nurse Boudreaux down a notch or two. Time for her to face reality, my reality. Before heading to the OR, I slip an extra sponge into my sleeve. It will be a shame when Nurse Boudreaux miscounts her sponges today. With the internal bleeding case it will be easy to slip into the abdomen while I am exploring to find the bleed.

Now, what you should know is that foreign objects, such as sponges, left in the human body after surgery can cause pain, infection, bowel problems (depending on the location of the surgery), additional and/or emergency surgeries, longer hospital stays, and in some cases, even death. The medical terminology when a sponge is retained in the body after surgery is called gossypiboma. It is more commonly referred to as textilioma. The effects may be noticed immediately, or they can take weeks, months or possibly even years to develop. Some of the ways gossypiboma presents itself is by a mass in the body or bowel tumor. It can be difficult to diagnose, with no clear evidence on x-ray, and can mask as an abscess.

***

Nurse Boudreaux is watching Dr. Habersham extremely close while he is scrubbing in. At the first sign that he is unfit to operate, she will speak up and not worry about the repercussions. She is not taking the heat for him being drunk. Observing the rules of sterility, she follows Dr. Habersham into the operating room by pushing the doors open with her rear, to avoid contaminating her hands. She wishes someone else was Dr. Habersham's assistant with this surgery. As the scrub nurse, she will be responsible for passing the instruments to him along with verifying that the number of instruments and sponges are the same before and after surgery.

She knows surgeons are a different breed of doctor. They can be self-critical and they expect just as much from the OR staff as themselves. Dr. Habersham takes it a step further at times. He yells, swears and throws instruments.

***

Mr. Bellue is strapped to the operating table to prevent him from falling off before or after anesthesia is administered. Nurse Boudreaux is meticulously counting sponges and instruments. She must ensure the same number is accounted once the surgery is complete. The anesthesiologist is busy preparing medications and equipment. His blood pressure and breathing will need to be monitored closely while under anesthesia.

Now that Mr. Bellue is under anesthesia, surgery can proceed. The anesthesiologist administers blood, fluid and blood pressure medication, which prevent a precipitous drop in blood pressure. A sterile green sheet is draped across Mr. Bellue, minus the window across his abdomen where the surgery is to be performed. His abdomen has been shaved and painted with iodine. Even though Mr. Bellue is a large man, you can visibly see his abdomen is distended. With one decisive stroke, I cut through the midline down to the final layer before entering the abdominal cavity. The cavity is swimming in dark, unclotted blood. There is a fair amount of bleeding. Surgical sponges are placed in the cavity while suction is being used to catch the overflow. The anesthesiologist is monitoring the blood pressure closely, in case there is a sudden drop. If this happens, he will have to push more blood and medication to maintain the patient's blood pressure. Once the sponges are packed into the abdomen the bleeding seems to be under control.

Currently the patient has had three units of red blood cells, and plasma has been administered. Clotting is improving. I am fairly certain I know where the bleed is, and it should be no problem confirming my belief. From the way the blood is pooling, the bleed is most probably coming from the spleen. Moving the sponges around, I do not detect any tumors. I find a fairly large laceration to the spleen. Instead of trying to repair the damage, I remove the spleen. Mr. Bellue can live without his spleen. It is a bystander organ with no significance. Mr. Bellue should lead a normal life. As I am removing the blood soaked sponges from Mr. Bellue's body, and Nurse Boudreaux is busy counting them, I make sure no one notices the sponge I slip into the abdominal cavity as I stitch him up. Now that I have left a sponge behind, Mr. Bellue will have problems with this more than he will with a missing spleen.

It ends up being a busy day in trauma. After a full day in the OR, I head to the doctor's lounge to work on my surgical notes before going home. By the time I finish, it is dark and a light mist is falling. Even though it is nighttime the damn bugs are still out. I will definitely need to get my car detailed tomorrow. There is only one person that I trust with that task, and he usually comes as soon as I call. It's too late to give him a call now, but first thing in the morning I will have him meet me at the hospital. I need to keep the

Aston looking good, plus I don't want the bug guts to eat at the paint. That wouldn't do at all. I make sure the car is kept in pristine condition at all times.

I take my usual route home. Since the radar detector is nice and quiet, I decide to punch it. I want to feel the power of the car. Moonlight reflects off of the wet road as the car speeds along. By the time I make it home, the mist had turned into a hard rain. I pull the car into the garage and stroll into the dark house. I'm too cheap to leave the lights on when I'm not home. I'm seldom here as it is. My current house is a plantation home that I have completely gutted and updated. I walk into my study and fix a scotch on the rocks. The house is exquisitely decorated, a showpiece. It's not me, though. I hired a decorator to furnish the house after the renovations were complete. The back of the house overlooks the Mississippi River. I still don't know what possessed me to let the contractor talk me into putting in a swimming pool, hot tub and "grillzebo". He convinced me that it would increase the value of the house. I didn't even know what a grillzebo was until he explained that it is a large gazebo with an outdoor kitchen built into it.

Now that the renovations are complete, I have considered selling the house and moving on to another project. The biggest problem I have to worry about is capital gains tax. I practically stole the rundown plantation several years back and began renovation. This purchase ignited a fire in the rumor mill at work; everyone wondered why I would want such a decrepit old house; there is no rumor mill more efficient than that of a hospital. Once all of the work was complete, the interior decorator used her connections and had the house featured in Architectural Digest and several other magazines. The house definitely fits the perceived lifestyle of a prestigious surgeon. The pictures of me show exactly how I want to look to the public; tall, suave, debonair and sophisticated. Exactly how a world class surgeon should look. Since I was a child, I dreamed of being famous. I have always craved, above all else, fame and notoriety. This article brings me one step closer. The picture I am most proud of is of me standing in my study with all my distinguished awards hanging on the wall behind my desk.

I turn on the television set to listen to the news. The weather forecast is on. As usual, it is going to be a hot, humid week. This is typical southern Louisiana weather. Once the news is over with, I walk back into my study and retrieve the newest of several brown leather binders on my bookcase. Each binder contains detailed journal entries of my experiments. I sit at my desk and update the latest entries. If my experiments are ever discovered, I will have to burn these binders. This may be the only solid proof of what I have done.

Feeling the fatigue of the workday, I turn off the lights downstairs and head for the stairs. The foyer is elegant and expansive, with a massive hardwood staircase that leads upstairs. When the house was remodeled, I had the carpenter combine several of the smaller rooms so that I could have a massive bath, closet and master bedroom. I also had him do this with the remaining rooms, but my master suite is palatial.

I walk into the bathroom and take a shower, washing off the remaining grime of the day and crawl into bed without a care in the world.

Chapter 26

The hospital administrator, Larry Stevens, calls me into his office first thing this morning. The first thought that goes through my mind is that Nurse Boudreaux must have turned me in for smelling of alcohol. This feels just like being called into the principal's office back in high school.

"Sit down Dr. Habersham. We need to talk about your behavior in the OR. I have had a few complaints from patients and their families lately that you seem to be too busy to talk to them before or after the surgery. You seem to always have a nurse or assistant surgeon do your pre and post op talks with the families and patients. There have also been numerous complaints about your behavior while you are operating. Several staff members have complained that you don't treat them with any respect; that you act like you are above them."

Now this pisses me off. "Let's face it, I am above them! They didn't go through medical school and residency to become a prestigious surgeon, I did. When I have a patient on the table, that person's life depends on me. The nurses have to do what I tell them, no questions asked. I cannot be held responsible because some nurse is overly sensitive."

Larry Stevens can see this conversation is getting him nowhere. "All I am asking is that you speak to the families of your patients and show the other staff a little compassion."

"I don't have time to worry about speaking to patients or families. As for the staff, I don't care about their feelings when I am in the operating room. I can't help it if they're too fragile to take criticism. If someone can't take the heat, then they need to find another career."

I believe it is time to give Nurse Boudreaux a little taste of her own medicine. I know she is the main one who complains about me.   If not her, then it was someone else that is a member of the operating room staff. I can be very vindictive when I want to be. I think it may be time to cause a few problems for them. I stop by the OR to look at the patients who are scheduled for surgery. Once I have the patient names memorized, I pull their charts, checking on their blood types. My plan is simple, to switch blood types so that a patient inadvertently gets the wrong blood.

I see a perfect case. A gentleman had banked his own blood prior to surgery. It is easy to switch the labels when no one is looking. This should keep the OR staff on their toes, and keep them off of my back for a while.

Chapter 27

Samuel Bellue is glad he is going home, but the searing pain seems to be worse than he expected. No matter what he takes or does, the pain doesn't resolve. The discharging physician, Dr. Henry Williams, informs him it is just inflammation from the surgical site, and in time it will heal and the pain will go away. Sam has been told the problem is fixed, but he feels worse than he did before surgery.

For several months after the surgery, the pain worsens. Sam is constantly having a low grade temperature, chills and nausea. One night the pain is so bad that he has to be brought to the emergency room. An x-ray is taken, and a foreign object is detected in his abdomen. Dr. Williams is the attending physician and schedules exploratory surgery first thing in the morning with the on call physician, Dr. Brad Griffith. Dr. Griffith removes a surgical sponge that was obviously left behind in the previous surgery. The sponge measures roughly fourteen by fourteen inches.

***

Dr. Griffith reviews the medical charts for Mr. Bellue's previous surgery and can't account for the missing sponge. It is necessary for the surgeons to rely on the nurses for accurate sponge counts before, during and after surgery. All Nurse Boudreaux's numbers matched before and after the operation. Dr. Griffith knows how meticulous Nurse Boudreaux is.   Had the sponge counts not matched, she would have asked for Dr. Habersham to not close until the discrepancy had been resolved. So, where the hell did this sponge come from then?

To make matters worse, the sponge has been rotting inside of Mr. Bellue. During surgery, it is found that the rotting sponge has caused damage to his intestines that is so severe, Dr. Griffith is forced to remove part of his intestines.

Dr. Griffith needs to bring this to the administrator's and Nurse Boudreaux's attention immediately. He is fairly certain a lawsuit will be filed. Mr. Bellue is not very happy when he is informed of the operation's outcome. While a sponge being misplaced during surgery may be very common, this is an extremely unusual case, because the sponge went undetected by Nurse Boudreaux and her sponge count matched before and after surgery. Could she have possibly miscounted? It's difficult to accept when someone you know makes a mistake, but sometimes mistakes do happen.

All departments of the hospital have a department head that bears the full responsibility for the affairs within that department. Usually this is a physician who has been appointed by the Board of Trustees. That department head's job description is fully detailed in the hospital's bylaws.

A hospital should run like a well-oiled machine. Most tragic occurrences in hospitals are more often due to a failure in the hospital system than physician error. Unfortunately, sometimes physicians and nurses do make medical errors. It is for this very reason that hospitals have a peer review committee set up. Each department head usually has a mandatory peer review in order to prevent these mistakes from happening. Deaths in the hospital will come under extremely heavy scrutiny from the peer review committee.

St. Anne's Hospital places their malpractice carrier on notice as soon as Dr. Griffith informs them of the possible mistake Nurse Boudreaux made during surgery. Since this incident resulted from surgery, the Department Head of Surgery will conduct the review. The surgical peer review committee comprises of five members who will review the surgical charts to see what further information is needed. They may either need a written statement from all staff present during the surgery, or a mandatory personal appearance.

***

Nurse Carol Boudreaux cannot believe what she is being accused of. She is extremely meticulous when counting the sponges and equipment before and after surgery. There is no way this could have happened when she was the nurse in charge. She has reviewed the surgical chart several times and the numbers match. There is no way she miscounted, especially since it's mandatory to count everything twice.

When she gets home, her husband is already there. He greets her with a hug as she enters the house through the garage. Giving him a quick kiss, she puts down her purse and keys. All she can think about is being in his arms and him making her feel safe and secure. Thankfully, Mark long ago accepted the long hours she works; although his office hours aren't exactly nine to five either. Mark is one of the best probate attorneys in town. She needs to talk to him about what has happened, to see if he feels they should get her an attorney. The hospital should protect her, but nowadays you never know what is going to happen. If they are trying to find a scapegoat, they could throw her to the wolves. She is relieved that she has her own malpractice insurance.

In all her years of nursing, she has never been brought before the committee. "Mark, I'm really worried. I didn't alter the charts. I counted what went in and out of that patient. I know I didn't miss anything."

"I'm sure the committee is going to see that the chart shows you did nothing wrong."

"That still doesn't explain how a sponge was left behind. I've never been reprimanded before. I hate that I may have a black mark on my record now."

"Relax for now. I don't think it is going to come to that."

"I don't know. Habersham will throw the blame on me. I think I pissed him off royally that day. He has been colder than normal since then. And there was the mix-up with the blood a while back. Even though the mistake was found to be the blood bank's fault, I feel as if Dr. Habersham has been watching my every move. They could even ban me from working on the surgical floor and make me recertify. What if they suspend my nursing privileges at the hospital? How will I ever find another nursing job?"

Mark and Carol mull over the possible outcomes for a while longer. "I love you and will stand by you no matter what. I don't think the committee will suspend you. They may give you a warning. All we can do is wait to see what happens. You need to try and get some sleep. Everything will work out sweetheart. You'll see."

They head to the bedroom. He held her hand as they
walked down the hallway, trying to give her some
reassurance.

***

Sam Bellue doesn't care who is to blame for the sponge
being left in him after surgery, he just knows that someone
is going to pay for his pain and suffering. The hospital bills
alone for the damage done to his body from the sponge are
piling up, not to mention all the time he has missed from
work.

Even though Sam is still in the hospital, the attorney he has
been speaking with has agreed to meet him here. Becky
Crosby comes highly recommended. He was told not to
underestimate her because she is female. She is supposed
to be tough as nails in the courtroom and doesn't take crap
off of anyone.

When she enters his room, she isn't anything like he was
expecting. She is a very tall, svelte woman. If he could
stand right now, they would probably see eye to eye, and
he is six feet tall.

"Mr. Bellue? I am Becky Crosby."

"Thank you for meeting me here. They said it will be at
least another week before I can go home. I'm not normally
one to believe in suing, but the bills are adding up, and I
keep hearing rumors that my boss is tired of all the time I
have had to take off of work. If I lose my job, then I will
have no money coming in. The internist I spoke with
yesterday doesn't know when I will be released to go back

to work either. The sponge did quite a number on my intestines. I may have to have another operation to fix some more damage; they are just waiting to see."

"This is going to be a very tricky case because you are an active patient right now. However, it won't be an impossible case. I usually instruct my patients not to talk to anyone about their case and to direct all the calls to me, but in this instance we can't do that. The hospital's attorney will also want to keep the doctors and staff from talking to you. Again, in this case it won't work.

I plan on putting the hospital and doctors here on immediate notice to get this ball rolling so to speak. Regardless of how the sponge got into your body, the hospital is at fault! Either the nurse, doctor or someone on staff here made the mistake. Thankfully, it was caught early enough; it could have been a fatal mistake."

"How long do you think it will be before we settle?"

"We don't want to settle too fast, since we don't know the extent of damage done to your body, but I don't foresee this being a long drawn out case. I doubt it will ever go to court. I honestly expect the hospital's insurance company to make an offer to settle once they receive my notice. They have no defense in the matter."

"That is the best news I have heard in a while."

Chapter 28

Dr. Jeffrey Cole just finished his exam of Jessica Stanford and will have to meet with her parents. He honestly can't believe he has another patient that had Dr. Habersham as their trauma surgeon who developed complications after surgery.

Little Jessica has complained of constant pain since her surgery. The little girl's foot resembles a club foot, but that isn't possible since those usually present at birth. Further evaluation will be needed.

 Once the x-rays and MRI's are complete, he discovers that Jessica has a bone missing from her ankle, causing her pain and hindering her ability to walk. It should have been obvious to Dr Habersham when he was repairing the ankle.

Dr. Cole plans on pulling several other patients' files that Dr. Habersham operated on in trauma to see if there is a pattern. This has to be more than a coincidence. Something fishy is going on, and if he is right, it will have to be brought to the hospital administrator's attention. Dr. Cole has never considered himself a "whistle blower", but if a surgeon is causing harm to patients, then he needs to be stopped. How many more patients of Dr. Habersham have developed problems after surgery, he wonders? What the hell is Habersham up to? Surely he isn't treating these patients like guinea pigs? If there is any inkling of truth to that statement, and the public becomes aware of it, all hell will break loose.   Putting aside medical ethics, why would a doctor even contemplate experimenting on his patients?

This isn't World War II, and we for sure aren't in a Nazi concentration camp. Jeffrey knows he will need documentation before he can accuse another doctor of unethical professional conduct. If Habersham is actually doing this, then surely he is covering his tracks. This really needs to be brought to Larry Steven's attention. Between the two of them, they can plan out what needs to be done. There is no way that this can be ignored if patients' lives are on the line.

Currently, all he can tell Larry is that he suspects something is wrong. He has no definite proof, but he suspects that Dr. Habersham did something malicious to Jessica Stanford's ankle; will he be able to prove it though?

***

"Mr. and Mrs. Stanford, thank you for meeting with me. I have reviewed your daughter's x-rays, and unfortunately we need to operate on her again."

Mrs. Stanford is definitely concerned. "I don't understand. I thought Dr. Habersham did an excellent job the first time."

Dr. Cole pulls up the films on his computer screen and points to the area of the missing bone in Jessica's ankle. "Can you see this small void here? This is where one of the ankle bones is supposed to be. For some reason, this was inadvertently missed during surgery. Now, unfortunately, without having the actual missing bone, I need to use an implant to "mimic" the portion of bone missing."

Dr. Cole can tell Mr. Stanford is furious. "What do you mean "inadvertently missed"? The trauma surgeon didn't realize he removed it?"

"That is what it looks like. For Jessica to ever walk right again, we will need to repair her ankle. Unfortunately, I cannot guarantee she will not have further problems. There is a good possibility she will need several more surgeries as she grows. Under normal conditions, her ankle bone would grow with her, but since we will be using an artificial bone, this is not going to happen. In order to keep up with Jessica's growth rate, we will need to replace the missing bone at several intervals during her growth spurts."

"How many surgeries are we talking about doctor?"

"I wish we could give you a definite answer, but I am hoping that by the time Jessica reaches twenty-one, she will no longer need any surgeries. Now, girls on average stop growing at the age of sixteen, so there is a chance that after that time she may not need any more corrective surgeries. Only time will tell."

Mrs. Stanford broke down in tears. "Now I wish I had never bought that damn trampoline for her."

Dr. Cole feels sorry for these parents. "Mrs. Stanford, you can't blame yourself for the accident. Now that we know what the problem is, I am hoping that we can correct the situation in the easiest way possible. I would like a colleague of mine to review Jessica's records and see if he has an alternative suggestion."

"Whatever you think is best. We just want you to correct this for Jessica. She is miserable and in so much pain."

Dr. Cole knows if he is right, little Jessica's pain is far from over. After reviewing several other patients' charts, Dr. Cole knows he will have to talk to Larry Stevens, and he set up an appointment to see him as soon as possible.

"Dr. Cole, what seems to be so urgent?"

"I wanted to talk to you about Dr. Habersham. A few things have come to my attention that I believe you should be made aware of. I believe Dr. Habersham is purposefully and maliciously causing harm to some of his trauma patients."

"Dr. Cole, as much as I dislike the man, that is a very serious accusation. Do you honestly believe a physician is deliberately harming patients?"

"I hope not, but the circumstances are peculiar. I believe there is enough evidence to warrant a peer review of the charts."

"We are talking about a prominent surgeon in this hospital. One who took the same Hippocratic Oath as you, I might add."

"I know, but Jessica Stanford's x-rays show that something horrible was done to her, and I believe he may have harmed several other patients during surgery as well."

* * *

After Larry Stevens reviews the charts, he knows this could be bad for the hospital, very bad indeed. He needs to call an emergency meeting with the Board of Directors. If this information is correct, then they need to pull Dr. Habersham's privileges before he can cause even more grievous harm to patients.

Larry knows he needs to talk to Habersham about the allegations, but he doesn't feel like dealing with any prima donna surgeon right now. Tomorrow will be soon enough to broach the subject with Habersham. The bastard will probably act self-righteous anyway.

"How many people have you talked to about this?"

"Other than informing Jessica Stanford's parents about the missing ankle bone, no one. I wanted to talk to you first."

"I wish you had talked to me before the Stanfords, but I understand you had a medical obligation to inform them. The fewer people we make aware of these suspicions, the better off we are. We don't want patients or the public catching wind of this. The medical malpractice suits that would ensue could be mind boggling, even if there is no wrongdoing. Hell, lately a doctor can look at a patient the wrong way and be sued. Damn lawyers."

"Do you know if any of the other hospitals Habersham worked at had any complaints?"

"He came highly recommended. Now I'm worried that maybe the previous hospitals gave him such glowing recommendations to get rid of him. Although, I have to say, this is the first time anyone has ever questioned his surgical skill. Character yes, skills no. I also plan on talking to a few of the surgical staff, to get their impression of Habersham, without divulging too much information as to why."

***

Later on that night, Richard and Eve Stanford are talking in bed. Richard still can't believe what Dr. Cole told them, "Eve, I know you don't want to hear this, but what if that doctor who operated on Jessica did this on purpose? I think we need to talk to a medical malpractice attorney to see what our options are. Somehow, some way, someone messed up; and we need to get to the bottom of this. Besides, it sounds like Jessica will need extensive medical care, and if it's the hospital or doctor's fault, then they should be forced to pay for it."

"I agree with you one hundred percent. They should be held accountable. What if this isn't the first time the doctor has done something like this?"

Chapter 29

Hillary Wells, Esquire, is the newest partner of Freeman, Smith & Wells. She likes the sound of that. The law office is located in the historic district of Springport. They dominate the top floor of the old Levingworth Building. The original building was built in the late 1800's, and Hillary is still in awe of the building's beauty after all the years of working here. Mr. Freeman wanted the law office to keep with the historic beauty of the building, and had it furnished with Chippendale antiques, as well as various other antiques. The hardwood floors were brought back to their original luster, as was the mahogany paneling. The wood gleams from the latest coats of wood polish, showing off the elegance of the office. Mr. Freeman wants their clients to feel comfortable, especially considering that they are paying an exorbitant hourly fee. Who would want to pay an attorney over $500 an hour if they worked in a hovel?

Hillary grew up a poor, white trash girl from a small town in Texas. She fought her way through poverty to become the newest partner in one of the most prestigious law firms in Louisiana. She can't wait to put an announcement in her hometown paper about her making partner. Let those assholes eat some crow for a change. All her life, everyone, even her teachers, said that she would never amount to anything, that she needed to accept her position in life and with her grades there was no way she would ever get a scholarship. That must have been the incentive that Hillary needed. She buckled down and brought her grade average up to a 4.0 during both her junior and senior year of high school. Still, the school counselor informed her that even with her grades as good as they were, she needed to focus on a community college. *"You know, Hillary, college is a lot harder than high school. You may have been able to bring your grades up, but honestly, maybe you should look at the local community college. The college curriculum is nothing like high school. I'm just worried that you won't be able to keep up with the other students."*

Well, Hillary has proven her wrong, too. Not only did she get a full scholarship to Loyola University, she graduated valedictorian.

During college, Hillary decided to focus on prelaw. She wanted to fight all the injustices in the world and becoming a lawyer was the best way she felt she could do this. Hillary had huge dreams all through college about what her life would be like, and now those dreams are coming to fruition. Here she is, in her corner office overlooking the mighty Mississippi River and sitting at her Chippendale desk. Instead of hanging her diplomas, pictures and various awards on the wall, she has strategically placed them along the massive, well lit bookshelf in the office. Hillary made sure the lights hit each award or picture perfectly. She is proud of all she has achieved so far and has no qualms about showing it off. The view from her office is breathtaking. On sunny afternoons the shimmering water from the Mississippi River helps her focus on whatever case she is working on. Watching the ships traveling up and down the river calms her nerves. It is the perfect office for her.

She notices that the river is especially busy today as she waits for her next client. Her law partners are just as excited about these new clients as she is. Richard and Eve Stanford are prominent citizens in the community. Richard Stanford is well known in the business community because of his financial success. If they could sway him to bring all his business over to their law firm, it would be a huge feather in their cap. The law firm has attorneys for all the various needs that arise for their clients. Unlike most law firms they do not limit their practice. She has wined and dined several prospective clients over the years, and has been quite successful at having them retain their law firm for all their legal needs. Since her arrival at Freeman & Smith, now Freeman, Smith & Wells, she has done absolutely nothing but enhance their reputation. Since the law firm was founded in 1935 she is the first person to ever make partner.

From what Hillary understands, Richard Stanford's current attorney only handles business litigation, and the Stanfords need an attorney to handle a personal matter. When Mrs. Stanford called to make the appointment, she was very secretive, and Hillary is intrigued. Mrs. Stanford informed Hillary they had met at a charity ball a couple of months back and she was impressed with her. She has a feeling that Hillary may be just the attorney they need. It seems as though Mrs. Stanford has already asked around town about her and has been informed that Hillary likes to play hardball. People shouldn't let Hillary's looks fool them; underneath that cool demeanor is a real bitch.

Hillary doesn't let what others think about her bother her. It is true that in court she is relentless. She shows no mercy to the defendant. That is the way it should be. One case at a time she is fighting the injustices of the world, or at least those that she can. She plays rough, and won't let her client take a small settlement offer just to keep from going to trial. Hillary loves to litigate cases, and going to trial doesn't scare her. That tenacity is what helped her make partner. She is the top litigation attorney here at the firm.

For this meeting she is wearing her best Versace suit and Christian Louboutin signature stilettos. She is dressed to impress. The suit not only screams money, but power as well. The exact statement she wants to make today.

Normally Hillary would meet new clients in her office, but her desk is still stacked high with files and law books from the current case she is working on. She was so focused this morning on the conference call from the defendant's attorney that she missed watching the might Mississippi Queen II passes by. The defense attorney desperately wants to settle, but they are nowhere near the amount Hillary has in mind for settling the case. She has to inform her client of the settlement offer, but she will push them as hard as she can to decline the offer. Hillary knows she can get a higher figure.

Hillary regrets missing the beloved steamboat pass by. Ever since she was a little girl the old steamboats fascinated her. One of her most cherished childhood memories is when she would go with her dad down to Louisiana and they would watch as the steamboats cruised along the river. They would fish for catfish, crab or whatever else was biting that day. Sometimes they would even come back with sacks of crawfish that they managed to catch. They would have a huge boil that night. As poor as they may have been her childhood was at least happy. Hillary decided to live in

Louisiana instead of Texas because of those childhood memories. Since her dad's passing, she feels closer to him here than she does back at home. She hopes that he is proud of her and what she has become. Hillary has been trying to talk her mom into moving here with her, but she refuses. All of her friends and what family is left are in Texas.

Hillary makes sure the secretary sets up the Waterford Crystal for the water and gorgeous set of Artistica Italian Deruta coffee cups. Hillary wants the conference room to impress but also make the Stanfords comfortable. Everything has to be perfect.

Her secretary buzzes her to let her know that the Stanfords are here. She goes out to the lobby to greet them personally. "Mr. and Mrs. Stanford, it is a pleasure to see you both again."

After they shake hands and finish the introductions, Hillary leads them back to the conference room. "I thought we would be more comfortable here than in my office."

Mr. Stanford is looking out the window at the picturesque view. "This is fine." He places his briefcase on the table and starts pulling out an enormous amount of paperwork. Hillary can't wait to see what this is about.

"Would either of you care for something to drink?"

Mrs. Stanford answers, "Coffee would be nice."

Hillary pours each of them a cup of coffee and places the cream and sugar within easy reach for them.

"Mrs. Stanford was quite secretive about the reason behind your needing to meet with me, so I've been intrigued as to what you need."

"The reason behind the veil of secrecy is that we didn't want anyone to get wind of what we have planned just yet. When our business attorney stated he didn't handle medical malpractice or personal injury cases, he suggested we look elsewhere. He wasn't sure how to handle the case, but suggested you. My wife remembered meeting you at a charity function, so here we are."

"What kind of case are you looking at then?"

"It is a medical malpractice case, but the doctor is a well-respected surgeon. Both my wife and I fear that if the hospital or doctor hear about the case, some records may be destroyed, hence the secrecy."

Now Hillary is very intrigued. "Do you honestly think the hospital would destroy the records?"

"I doubt the hospital would, but I have no doubt the doctor may try something. Dr. Jeffrey Cole has been extremely helpful in obtaining the documentation you may need. He is actually the one that suggested we contact an attorney. I also feel that something needs to be done about this doctor before he harms another patient."

"Let me get some background information from you."

"Our daughter had broken her ankle, and had to have emergency surgery. Dr. Habersham performed the surgery at St. Anne's. After the cast was removed, she started physical therapy. By this time, she was seeing Dr. Cole, who is an orthopedist. Dr. Cole wanted to wait a little longer before removing the pins in her ankle. He wanted to make sure the bone had healed correctly and physical therapy was needed since she was still having trouble walking. Jessica constantly complained about the pain in her ankle, but we figured it was from all the hardware in her ankle and the fact that her bones were trying to mend. As time passed, we noticed that her ankle was turning in and not growing correctly. Actually, it was the physical therapist that noticed it. Dr. Cole did an x-ray of Jessica's ankle and found that one of her ankle bones is missing. The x-rays prior to surgery show the bone in place. Dr. Cole believes that Dr. Habersham intentionally removed the bone from Jessica's ankle during surgery."

As Mr. Stanford talked, all Hillary could see was dollar signs in her eyes. This case could be huge.

"And Dr. Cole has evidence that this was done deliberately?"

"I believe he does."

Hillary can't wait to take this case on. This is just the kind of case she went to law school for, but she does need to warn them these are not easy cases. "Let me start off by saying that this does sound like a very interesting case. However, medical malpractice cases are not easy cases to win. It will take some tenacity and perseverance."

"From what I understand, you are the best attorney for this case."

"I agree, and I do not back away from cases. I do need to warn you though, that these particular cases are not cheap to try. First off, jurors don't like to hear that doctors or hospitals make mistakes. To prove our case, I will not only need the medical records and Dr. Cole's testimony, but also an expert witness. The expert witness will need to send me a detailed report confirming the medical malpractice so that I can have it on file.

Also, you will not get rich from a medical malpractice case. You will be able to recoup medical expenses and lost wages, but there is a cap on the tort amount you can receive from punitive damages. It is set at $250,000. This is regardless of what the jury awards you."

"Ms. Wells, money is not the reason my wife and I are even exploring this venue. This doctor knowingly set out to harm my daughter. How many others has he harmed? How many more does he plan on harming? He has to be stopped! The public needs to be made aware of what he has done. Jessica will have to endure numerous surgeries until she is through growing. This will be painful and there is no telling what the future will hold for her. She will never be able to join in the same activities as her friends while growing up. The doctor isn't sure what her childhood will be like. This case sets a new precedent for the medical books. Dr. Cole has not found a case where a child has intentionally had a bone removed from her ankle during surgery for no reason. They are not even sure if the artificial bone will work. Only time will tell."

"Mr. Stanford, as long as you and your wife understand what all is entailed in this case and you are both in agreement, I say let's go for it. I also believe this doctor needs to be stopped. I would suggest not only do we file a medical malpractice case, but we also need to inform the state licensing board about what is happening. It will help strengthen our case if they investigate the matter also. By filing a medical malpractice claim, we only hurt the doctor financially, but by bringing this to the State of Louisiana Medical Licensing Board's attention, they can revoke his license, so he can no longer practice medicine in this state. Another avenue we may want to pursue is talking to the district attorney. If we can show harmful intent, a criminal case could possibly be brought against the doctor."

Mr. Stanford is impressed, very impressed. He has no doubts whatsoever that they did indeed find the right attorney. "Ms. Wells, I must say, I like the way you think."

"I do need to warn you that I do not come cheap. My set fees for personal injury and medical malpractice cases are thirty-three percent if we settle before trial and forty percent if I have to go to trial. Also, you should know that the trial does not scare me. I love to litigate cases and most defense attorneys know it. The fees do not include costs, which will also come out of the settlement amount. Expert witnesses are not cheap and charge an hourly rate. I will also need to pay the expert witness a retainer fee before he will even look at the case. The firm does not require a retainer from you; we front all the costs before trial."

"As I am sure you are aware, money is no object to us. If we need to pay for the expert witness up front, we will."

"Let's keep this case as if you were one of our regular clients please. I would prefer it not look as though the plaintiff is paying the expert witness directly."

"I understand completely. Just tell me what you need us to do."

"It is going to be imperative that you not speak with anyone about this case. I want to have the element of surprise when I file the case."

"The only two people that know are my business attorney and Dr. Cole. I'm not worried about either of them talking."

"Good. Very good indeed. I already have an expert witness in mind that I would like to use. I will need to inquire as to whether or not he is friends with Dr. Habersham. Dr. Habersham is well known in the surgical field, so that may cause a problem in finding an expert witness."

As soon as the Stanfords leave, Hillary calls Dr. Kenneth Brown to see if he has heard of Dr. Anthony Habersham before. "Dr. Brown, this is Hillary Wells. I have a case I am working on and was wondering if you had ever heard of a Dr. Habersham."

"I've never met the man personally, but I have heard his name mentioned a few times. May I ask why?"

"I would rather discuss this with you in private if that is okay? Is there a good time that we can meet?"

"Actually, I am free today at lunch if you would like to meet."

"That sounds good. Let's meet at Clementine's. I will ask for a quiet table so we can talk in private."

"Sounds like this could be an interesting case then. I can't wait to meet with you."

Chapter 30

It has been several months since Jude Hudson had his gall bladder removed and he is feeling worse than before. He has even had to miss a good bit of football practice and now that football season is getting ready to start up he isn't ready to play. His coach has insisted he see another doctor for a more detailed follow-up. Something is definitely going on. He can barely hold down food and he is losing weight. In his profession that is not good.

His coach scheduled an appointment with an internist, Dr. Brian Harris. Jude is nervous about the appointment and is glad that he doesn't have a long wait. "Mr. Hudson, I understand that you still aren't feeling well after your gallbladder surgery."

"Yes sir. I have been having problems with nausea, vomiting, loss of appetite, abdominal pain and a low-grade fever that comes and goes. I was told my recovery time would only be a couple of weeks."

"The first thing we need to do is an endoscopic ultrasound to check and see if there may be some scar tissue or possibly an injury to a bile duct. Initially, if a bile duct is injured the patient may notice that they're not feeling well, but eventually they will become jaundiced and the liver will stop functioning. So far I see no signs of jaundice, but I do want to rule out that the bile duct was cut. Leakage of bile can cause symptoms of pain and breathing difficulties. There are serious consequences of a bile leak. It can even poison the body and possibly lead to death. Due to the symptoms you are presenting with, I believe we need to investigate quickly.

"Wouldn't the surgeon have noticed if he cut a bile duct though?"

"I was informed that this was a simple procedure and that there shouldn't be any problems."

"Normally laparoscopic gallbladder surgery is a safe procedure. Unfortunately, mistakes can happen, putting the patients at risk and causing serious harm. Complications can occur with any surgery. If I am correct and the bile duct was damaged during the surgery, subsequent corrective surgery will be needed. There is a chance you may have permanent pain and/or digestive problems. I also need to rule out cholangitis, an infection or inflammation of the bile ducts, causing bacteria and other waste products in the small intestine to flow upward causing infection. Cholangitis can be life threatening if left untreated."

***

I've just entered the hospital for my shift when Larry Stevens calls. "I need you in my office now."

"I just got to the hospital."

"You have five minutes to get up here."

I can't help but wonder what crawled up Larry Stevens' ass. He can be a real pain at times.

"Please have a seat Dr. Habersham. I just got off the phone with a Dr. Brian Harris. He is currently treating Jude Hudson, whom you performed a gall bladder operation on. We had a very interesting telephone conversation in which he wanted to let me know my surgeon screwed up royally."

I have been wondering what became of that patient; if someone had figured out he had a bile duct cut during the operation. "What mistake are you talking about?"

"Dr. Brian Harris is accusing you of cutting the bile duct on Jude Hudson. The man has been diagnosed with cholangitis. Treatment has been started, but he fears it may have been started too late. There is quite a bit of damage already."

"The patient should have presented to a doctor when the symptoms first appeared. I don't see how I can be blamed for his delay in medical treatment."

"You can't be serious? Regardless if the man delayed medical treatment or not, there is no denying the bile duct was cut during surgery. You are a better surgeon than that. That is a mistake an intern may make, but not an accomplished surgeon."

"And what if it wasn't a mistake?"

"I hope I misunderstood you? What else could it be other than a mistake?"

"I do not make mistakes, Mr. Stevens!"

"What have you done? Do you realize the ramifications that will face not only you, but the hospital? This man is a local hero and the community will be outraged. The damage this will do to the reputation of our hospital may be irreparable."

"I still don't see how this is my problem."

"You don't, do you? You do realize Dr. Harris will report his findings to the state's medical licensing board. The call he made to me was a courtesy call. Thanks to you there is a huge chance the hospital will be crucified."

"What ever happened to innocent until proven guilty?"

"You don't understand, do you? Dr. Harris has the evidence proving the cut bile duct."

"But it has to still be proven that I did it. What if the bile duct was cut afterwards, or maybe an accidental cut that was missed during the surgery?"

***

Larry Stevens runs his hands through his hair. Talking to this man is like talking to a brick wall. On top of this blatant malpractice situation, there are the other cases Dr. Cole has brought to his attention. He feels as if he is on a ship that is sinking fast, very fast. "I am going to have to inform the Board of Directors about this. There will be an investigation into the matter. There is a chance that the peer review committee will go over all of your surgeries since you started here. Is there a chance they will discover something else that I need to be made aware of?"

***

"Go ahead. I have nothing to hide. I am a very accomplished surgeon." There is no way they can find out about my research projects. I am not worried in the least. I am smarter than any of the doctors that they will use to review my surgical records. Besides, most of the experiments can easily be blamed on something else.

Chapter 31

As I leave for the hospital this morning, I notice it looks as if it's is going to be a gorgeous day. It has been uncharacteristically quiet in the trauma center at St. Anne's lately. For a while it seemed as if the trauma patients were coming in one right after another, but the last couple of days the trauma cases have just trickled in. Could this be the calm before the storm? The OR has been busy, but mostly with elective surgeries. I crave the unknown and would probably go crazy seeing the same patients and cases day in day out. Most of the surgeons operating today are the ones that prefer a nine to five practice so they can keep their Saturdays open for golf. Golf is not something I am particularly fond of. Several of the nurses have commented on how much they are enjoying this current hiatus. Not me though, I crave the rush. I feel my skills grow stagnant when we have a lull in patients.

As much as I love pushing my Aston Martin to its limits, I decide to take a leisurely drive to the hospital. There is no rush getting there, no trauma cases are waiting for me. Even the traffic is light for this time of the morning.

With the current lull at the hospital, the rumor mill has been churning more than usual. I have been hearing rumors going around that Dr. Jeffery Cole requested several patients' charts that I operated on. Could he be on to my little experiments, or is it a conspiracy between Stevens and Cole. Maybe I'm just being paranoid and neurotic? I need to get my emotions in check, only a fool lets emotions influence their judgment. I have come too far to let some wannabe surgeon think he can outsmart me.

My life has always been full of adversity. After all, I do have a life that others are jealous of. Is this possible; do I have to worry about the hospital staff conspiring against me? The very thought is crazy to say the least, but why would Dr. Cole need to request to see these surgical charts? There is no way anyone has figured out what I have been doing.

Later on that day, the rumors are confirmed when Larry Stevens calls me up to his office. "Dr. Habersham, it has come to our attention that you may have performed an unauthorized procedure on a young trauma patient. After much discussion with the Board of Directors, I have been asked to personally hand deliver this letter to you. I will also need you to sign and acknowledge that you have received said letter.

"This is fucking bullshit, and you know it!"

"Until the peer review committee has reached a decision, my hands are tied. This is being done to protect the hospital's interests. I'm sure you understand."

Dr. Habersham:

Issues relating to patient care have been brought to the Board of Directors' attention. A review by the peer review committee has been ordered. Due to the serious nature of these allegations of misappropriate patient care, until said review is complete, the Board of Directors has passed a motion that your actions in the hospital are to be closely monitored. The monitoring will be carried out as stated below:

*•	All procedures performed by you in the hospital will be monitored.*

*•	The Chief of Surgery, or his designee, will be your monitor.*

*•	All nurses and surgical staff have been informed that no case will proceed without the assigned monitor in attendance.*

*•	You will not jeopardize patient or staff safety. Cases will be closely reviewed.*

*•	Monitoring will continue until a decision has been reached by the peer review committee.*

Any questions can be directed to Larry Stevens, Hospital Administrator.

I am fuming by the time I finish the letter. "A fucking babysitter! Are you serious? I refuse to be monitored."

Larry Stevens smiles. "That is your decision, but if you refuse to be monitored, then you will be banned from the OR and this hospital until the peer review committee has reached their decision. This monitoring is in no way a disciplinary action, but rather an investigative activity, to protect all of our interests in this matter. It is designed to evaluate the surgical procedure you are performing and to confirm that no questionable or unauthorized procedures are taking place."

"And so what if I am doing unauthorized procedures on patients? The hospital has as much culpability as me."

"Dr. Habersham, are you informing me that you DID indeed perform an unauthorized procedure on this or any other patient?"

"I am not confirming or denying anything. Just asking what if I did? The hospital has as much culpability as me."

"Dr. Habersham, I repeat, are you informing me that you DID indeed perform an unauthorized procedure on this patient?"

"I am not confirming or denying anything. Just asking what if I did?"

Larry Stevens can't believe the arrogance of this man. "Then I would have to let the Board of Directors know immediately."

***

Larry Stevens is glad to be leaving the hospital for the day. It has been a hell of a day. After the conversation he had with Dr. Habersham today, he knows that tomorrow is going to be just as bad. He will have to meet with the Board of Directors to inform them about his conversation, along with the legal department and maybe even the malpractice carrier. Crap, this is not what he needs.

He aims his remote control at his car and pushes the button. The doors unlock and he hurries into the car. He recently bought the Lexus LS460. After years of scrimping and saving he finally rewarded himself with the car. He paid cash for the car, and loves his new indulgence. He pulls the door shut and listens as the car door makes a solid thud. The car is not only luxurious, but it has great safety features. After seeing so many severely injured patients come into the emergency room doors from car accidents, he wanted to make sure his next vehicle had a high safety rating and being a luxury vehicle. He takes a deep breath, and enjoys the new car smell. Even the leather seats are exquisite. This car was definitely worth the money. The engine springs to life effortlessly. It drives and handles like a dream.

On his way home, he thinks life was so much simpler when he first started this job. Now, because of the decisions of one surgeon, the hospital may be forced into bankruptcy. The financial ramifications could be astronomical due to one man's incompetency. There has to be some way to protect the hospital. How many patients has Habersham experimented on in the past? He hopes it is just the one, but if Dr. Cole is correct in his assumptions, it is more than any of them want to know about. Then they have this whole business with Jude Hudson to worry about.

Chapter 32

Hillary Wells is ready to file the medical malpractice lawsuit against Dr. Anthony Habersham. All her medical expert witnesses have submitted their reports and she finalized the motion last night. It has taken maniacal preparation to get everything ready, but she is confident in filing the case. There is no doubt in her mind that it is a slam dunk of a case.

The defense has a hell of a case to defend. She wonders if they are going to find an expert witness to rebut her expert witnesses' testimony. It is highly unlikely. Usually it only takes a slightly different interpretation of the medical records to establish a credible defense, but she has a feeling that it will take a good bit of effort to find an expert witness to help the defense. She had previously let the doctor and hospital know of the pending lawsuit, to see if any settlement offer would be made. Surprisingly, the claims adjuster for the hospital's insurance carrier made a policy limits offer in hopes of "sparing the family from the heartache of a trial". Hillary suspects it has to do with the fact they want the matter closed as soon as possible. However, the good doctor never acknowledged the pending lawsuit. The Stanfords never wanted retribution from the hospital, so they accepted their offer; but they do want to pursue the case against Dr. Habersham, which is fine with Hillary. She can't wait to litigate this case.

The first thing she plans on doing is deposing Dr. Habersham. She can't wait to get the man under oath and question him. Dr. Brown's report is very damning and it will feel good taking him down.

Chapter 33

I am sitting at home early one morning when the doorbell rings. *Now who on earth can that be?* I never have visitors, and the reason I like living where I do is because the neighbors are all busy with their own lives and keep to themselves.

Standing at the door is an older gentleman, "Dr. Habersham?"

"Yes, what I can I do for you? How did you find my address?"

He hands me a document and states, "This is for you. You have been served." Then he turns and walks away.

Damn it, he's a process server. Of all the rotten luck! After all the years I have been practicing medicine and performing my little experiments, this is the first time I have been sued in a medical malpractice case. When I see the patient's name, I know it isn't good. I have been hearing rumors around the hospital that the little girl's parents are upset.

The little girl's foot has not grown right since the surgery, growing more like a club foot than her normal foot. She also has problems bearing any weight on it, and when she does, it is constantly straining the ankle bones and causing excruciating pain. This is the one case that may actually hurt my career. The parents are asking for $500 million dollars. This amount is more than my medical malpractice insurance covers. If I lose the case, it will bankrupt me. The hospital has not been named as a co-defendant, which can only mean that they have already settled. My only chance of not bearing any financial damage was if they hospital had been named in the lawsuit; they at least have deeper pockets than me.

My hands are shaking with fury. I cannot believe one of my experiments has been found out and now I am being sued. If those damn parents had never bought the little girl a trampoline, then none of this would have ever happened. Of all the rotten luck!

Now, on top of everything else, I have to deal with the peer review committee and the insurance company. My fate is in their hands. I will have to report this immediately to my malpractice carrier. I wonder if Larry Stevens knows about the lawsuit.

After speaking to my insurance carrier, I show up for work as if nothing has happened. Later on that afternoon, I receive a call from a Joseph Hoffpauir, informing me that his firm, Hoffpauir and Whittington, will be representing me in the lawsuit. They need to meet with me at nine a.m. sharp the following day. I inform them that if I have no trauma cases, I will be there. I am politely informed to get another doctor to cover my morning. And so it begins. I do not like being told what to do.

I have to dig down deep inside myself to find the strength to deal with this mess. I refuse to let this one case control my life. In a way, I want this case resolved now, but I also don't want to admit to any wrong doing. I have to tread carefully, because if I put up too much of a fight, then someone will want to examine all my patient records with a fine tooth comb. There is a chance that if they look hard enough, they will find what I don't want them to.

Paul Whittington greets me the next morning. After a long discussion between the partners, it was decided Paul would be better to take on this case.

As it turns out, Paul has had better luck going up against the plaintiffs' attorney in court. As long as my attorney wins, I don't care who represents me.

"Well, let's get right down to business, shall we. I must warn you that the plaintiff's attorney, Hillary Wells, is a talented attorney. Not only is she smart, she is also committed to any case she is working on. She shows no fear, and has no qualms about going to court."

"Is that your way of informing me she is out of your league?"

"No. Out of all the attorneys in this law firm, I have had the best success when going up against her. She does not like to settle though, and loves to take cases to trial. Also, she does not take frivolous lawsuits, so she must know she has a winner. I already have a copy of the medical records in question. I must say, I am impressed with your documentation, and it looks like your young patient was provided with excellent medical care. However, I don't see any notations about the possibility of missing a bone. How do you explain the fact that the patient had no previous medical problems, and there is now a bone missing after you performed surgery on her? I see where Dr. Cole has noted that x-rays are conclusive, and a bone is missing"

"It is missing from the original surgery."

"I don't understand then. Did someone not inform the parents a bone was missing from the little girl? From the previous medical records, there is no mention of a club foot or other problems. Her pediatric checkups before the surgery were all normal."

"No, that would be correct. Before the accident, I am sure she was a picture of health with a perfect little ankle."

"Dr. Habersham, what am I missing then? I am trying to reconstruct this case the best I can."

"I purposely left out the bone in her ankle, to see what would happen.   Call it a little experiment if you like?"

"Wait a minute! Are you telling me you purposely meant to commit medical malpractice on this little girl's ankle when you operated on her?"

"Yes, that is exactly what I am saying. I wanted to see if the ankle would grow right if an integrate part was missing. I got my answers. Turns out the ankle grew almost the same as a club foot would."

"Dr. Habersham, do you understand what you are telling me?"

"I do. Do you comprehend what I am telling you?"

"I'm afraid I do. You butchered this poor little girl to satisfy some perverse curiosity!"

"I don't know if I would describe it exactly like that, but basically yes."

✳✳✳

Paul Whittington is utterly dumbfounded. This doctor admitted to medical malpractice. There is no way this can go to trial. He will need to talk with the carrier and settle this case as quickly as possible. There is no way this doctor has coverage limits that will cover the medical expenses as well as pain and suffering. They are screwed.

"Dr. Habersham, I need to talk with your insurance carrier so that we can strategize the best way to handle this case. In the meantime, I need a copy of your curriculum vitae. There are also some more forms that I need you to take home and fill out. If you can return them as quickly as possible it will be greatly appreciated. "

"I'll get the papers back to you as soon as possible."

Paul Whittington isn't sure he wants to ask this next question, "Dr. Habersham, are there other patients that you have experimented on?"

"But of course there are."

"I see. Have you ever been sued before for medical malpractice?"

"No, this is my first time."

"Well, do you have any idea how many patients you have experimented on?"

"Oh, dozens, I would have to check my journals to give you an exact number."

"I'm going to need that information, as well as their names."

"I must warn you, I don't want this information shared with anyone else. This is the first patient where two and two have been put together. "

"You mean to tell me that none of the others have noticed?"

"If they were noticed, I was never brought into the mix, until now. One guy died in the hospital for MRSA, but the hospital settled that wrongful death suit right away. No one ever realized I was the one who intentionally infected him with the MRSA bacteria. Another patient, Jude Hudson is just starting to put things together. Larry Stevens, the hospital administrator, informed me the other day that the patient found out I cut his bile duct during surgery. However, the patient is under the impression that this was an accident."

Paul is going to have to sit down with his partner and discuss this case thoroughly. The liability alone is enormous.   What have they gotten themselves into this time?

"Dr. Habersham, I am going to stress that you don't talk to anyone about this case or any of your other patients. This will also include your malpractice carrier. Is that clear?"

"Crystal."

"I'm quite sure the hospital administrator will try to draw you into a conversation. Don't talk to him either."

"Don't worry, Larry Stevens won't talk to me. Neither of us likes the other."

"Perfect. Let's keep it that way then. You should also know I represent you, but I am being paid by your insurance carrier. Your coverage limits are not going to be high enough, so you will need to hire your own attorney to protect your personal assets. You are only protected up to three million dollars."

"I don't see where we are going to need more than that. I personally don't plan on settling."

Paul has a feeling this is going to be a very difficult client. Janet Overton is the adjuster working the case for Liberty Medical. Now that Dr. Habersham has left, he needs to call her.

"Janet, it's Paul Whittington. I need to arrange a meeting between you, your supervisor and our firm. I just met with Dr. Habersham and the news isn't good."

"How soon do you want to meet?"

"Yesterday if possible. The doctor admits he knew he was committing malpractice, and did it intentionally to cause harm to the little girl."

"Please tell me you aren't serious?"

"I wish I wasn't. It gets worse though, she's not the first one."

Janet cringes when she hears the news. "Oh my God. This is disastrous."

"He doesn't want to settle either."

"It doesn't matter if he wants to settle or not, we won't pay more than his coverage limit if he goes to court and loses. He doesn't have a choice in that matter. Let's do a telephone conference first thing in the morning. Is eight o'clock good for you?"

"Perfect. We need to formulate a strategy."

***

Janet definitely needs to talk to her supervisor. Unfortunately, the way the insurance policy is written, they can't settle the case unless the doctor agrees. The one good thing is that if they do go to trial and lose, they are only liable for the policy limits; the good doctor is liable for the remainder. This is not a case any of them want to see go to trial though. This damn doctor is going to come across looking like Dr. Frankenstein. On top of that, if this suit catches the public's attention, which it most likely will, then there are sure to be more malpractice cases filed. This may turn into a freaking nightmare that could bankrupt them.

***

Paul Whittington sets up another meeting with Dr. Habersham to discuss the possibility of a settlement. "Dr. Habersham, thank you for meeting with me. It is my professional opinion that we need to discuss a settlement offer. The plaintiff's attorney is experienced in medical malpractice, and she is out for blood. We are going to be taking a huge chance if this goes to trial. I believe we can get them to accept a fair settlement amount. You need to take into consideration that if we go to trial and lose, you will be liable for any amount over your policy limit of three million dollars."

"No! I do NOT want to settle."

"I had a feeling you were going to say that. As your attorney, I am obligated to tell you I think you are making a huge mistake. This case could very well bankrupt you. There is no denying you did this on purpose, you said so yourself. The jurors are going to find in favor of the plaintiff. This is a very young child who will have multiple surgeries for several more years. Not only will she have several expensive and painful surgeries, there is no guarantee that this will make her quality of life any better."

I can't help but be angry at this man. He is trying to push me into settling a case that I don't want to settle. "I am telling you, I do not want to settle. What I did may be construed by some as malevolent, but it was for my research. Surgeons will only get better if they push themselves, and that is what I did each time I experimented on a patient. It was a cause and effect experiment on her. Now I know what will happen if a bone is removed from a child's ankle. Besides, if the parents hadn't been so neglectful and let her jump on a trampoline without safety netting, then none of this would have happened to their precious daughter. This is their fault."

Paul can't believe his ears. This doctor is putting the blame on the parents. There is no way this man can ever take the witness stand. The plaintiff's attorney will slaughter him. The man in front of him is cool, detached, professional and possibly insane. How can anyone openly admit they experimented on patients they have operated on? Legal ramifications aside, this doctor is a nightmare. He could make anyone question whether or not to trust any doctor.

"If you refuse to settle, then I will need to set up an appointment so I can prep you for trial. The plaintiff's witness list is impressive. She has several top notch expert witnesses lined up to testify against you."

"I'm not worried about what my peers have to say about me."

"Well, you should be. I have a feeling they are going to crucify you on the witness stand. Another problem is that I won't have any expert witnesses to disqualify anything the plaintiff's expert witnesses have to say, because there are none. Every expert witness I have talked to agrees with the plaintiff's expert witnesses. Everyone I have spoken to finds your actions so abhorrent and the evidence so damning they refuse to attempt to assist in your defense."

"What I did to these patients was for research! With each experiment, I was trying to ascertain the outcome of a medical experiment."

"Dr. Habersham, what you did was use human beings as test subjects, without their knowledge. They did not give their consent to be a part of your barbaric experiments. There will be serious repercussions from this. Did you ever have any misgivings about conducting your so called experiments?"

"Of course not! These were simply research projects. If a patient died, then that was of no consequence to me. I was in a hospital, and plenty of test subjects were available."

"This is completely insane! You cannot treat patients as your own personal lab rats."

"I had questions that I needed answers to in order to further my knowledge of the human body. These experiments helped me ascertain those answers. We may never know if these experiments will one day benefit an injured person."

"These experiments, as you call them, were done to satisfy some sick and perverse need inside you and nothing more. Do you not believe in the sanctity of human life?"

"In each situation, I had a hypothesis and needed an answer. The end justifies the means! The pursuit of the truth is the ultimate justification for my experiment as I see it."

"Not only is it illegal, but utterly and completely immoral to experiment on human beings without their knowledge or permission. Do you not comprehend this fact at all?"

"Please, scientists have experimented on animals for years against their will. If the doctors hadn't experimented on patients then there would be no organ transplants or chemotherapy for cancer patients. Besides, I do not need to sit here and listen to you lecture me about morality. Your job is to defend me to the best of your ability in this case and that is it!"

This new client of his is truly an insufferable bastard. There is no way there will be a good outcome to this.

Chapter 34

Just when I thought my day couldn't get any worse, I checked my mail. A letter from the Medical License Board was awaiting me.

Dear Dr. Habersham:

Issues relating to the possible misappropriate patient care of Jude Hudson and a minor, Jessica Stanford; have been brought to our attention. You have twenty days from receipt of this letter to send in a written response to the allegations contained herein regarding the medical treatment for Jude Hudson and the minor patient Jessica Stanford.

It has been alleged that you intentionally and knowingly cut the bile duct while performing gallbladder surgery on Jude Hudson.

It has been alleged that you inappropriately removed a part of Jessica Stanford's ankle bone causing a malformation of her ankle. Due to the malformation of said ankle, several corrective surgeries will be needed as the child grows.

Jessica Stanford's parents allege that you failed to inform them of any modifications performed on their daughter's ankle during surgery. Failure to get informed consent of the minor's parents was inappropriate as well as performing an unnecessary procedure on said minor.

Upon review of the patient's chart, there is no documentation of said procedure…..

This is just what I needed to end an already bad day. As much as I dislike the attorney handling the medical malpractice lawsuit, I will need to see if he can address this matter as well. My once brilliant career may be on its way down the drain, all because a patient's parents could not handle the fact that their daughter had an unauthorized procedure done on her ankle. If they hadn't been so irresponsible in buying her that damned trampoline, none of this would have occurred.

Chapter 35

Paul Whittington receives the Notice of Deposition late in the day. Crap. He knew the plaintiff's attorney would want to depose Habersham. He knew from experience that Hillary Wells would not be sending any settlement demands and was moving towards a trial. Habersham is going to crucify himself. Not only does he refuse to let a settlement offer be made, but there will be no denying the malpractice if this deposition takes place.

Paul Whittington has his secretary call Habersham to set up an appointment to prepare him for his deposition.

"Dr. Habersham, a deposition is really no big deal. You will be asked a number of questions about the surgery and the treatment you performed on the plaintiff. I need you to answer as simply and honestly as you can. Do not divulge any additional information. Do not express your opinion at all! Most importantly, only answer the question you are asked. Do not go off on a tangent. I cannot express that fact enough. DO NOT GO OFF ON A TANGENT ABOUT ANYTHING! Keep your answers brief and to the point.

I will be right there by your side. After the plaintiff's attorney asks you a question, I need you to delay your answer briefly. This is in case I feel the question is inappropriate. If the question is inappropriate, I will make an objection and instruct you not to answer the question. If I do object to the question, it is imperative that you do NOT answer.

I also need you to make sure you understand the question being asked. Listen carefully to what the plaintiff's attorney is asking you. If at any time you do not understand a question, say so. Once you are sure you understand what the question is, and I have NOT objected to the question, you can then answer."

***

I am sitting here listening to this attorney, but the whole time I feel like this is a waste of my time. "This is a joke, this whole thing is ridiculous. I don't need some attorney telling me how to answer questions."

"Dr. Habersham, I can assure you this is no joke. I need you to be careful about how you answer your questions. If you inform the plaintiff's attorney you deliberately removed a piece of that little girl's ankle bone, she will hang you out to dry in court. Do you understand this?"

"I understand completely. I just don't see why we have to do this whole dammed deposition thing. Let's just get on with the trial."

"This is all part of the trial process. There is only one way we can avoid the deposition. Let me make a settlement offer to the plaintiff in the amount of policy limits."

"No! I refuse to allow a settlement offer. That is the end of this discussion."

***

Paul Whittington can feel a headache coming on fast. No amount of pain killers will cure this headache. It will be with him until this nightmare trial is concluded. Damned obnoxious, narcissistic client.

Prior to this case, Paul actually enjoyed practicing law. However, this case has him rethinking his decision to become a defense attorney. He has sometimes wondered if his clients were actually guilty, but it makes his skin crawl that he has to represent a client that admits his guilt and has no remorse about it.

***

The day of the deposition has finally arrived. Once pleasantries are exchanged, I take the oath and the plaintiff's attorney dives right in. The beginning of the deposition goes smoothly. Hillary Wells asks me about education, where I went to college, medical school, internship and finally residency. This all seems quite mundane to me. It is going to be a long day if this is how a deposition goes.

***

Paul Whittington can feel the pit in the bottom of his stomach grow larger by the minute. So far the deposition is going good, but he knows the other shoe is going to drop at any moment. Paul has already talked to several expert witnesses and they have all concluded the same thing; that what Dr. Habersham did is criminal, if not medical malpractice and possibly insanity. Why did the insurance company have to write that clause into their policy that the doctor had to approve a settlement?

Paul can tell that Hillary is winding down on her background questions. "Dr. Habersham, why did you operate on Jessica Stanford?"

Paul looks over at Dr. Habersham, this is when the other shoe is going to drop; he can feel it in his bones. "Jessica Stanford fell off of a trampoline and broke her ankle. I was called in as a trauma surgeon since the orthopedic surgeon was busy operating on another patient."

***

Hillary has been waiting for this line of questioning since the deposition began. She can't wait to see how the "good doctor" tries to squirm his way out of this. "Dr. Habersham, did you consciously decide to remove a portion of Jessica Stanford's ankle bone?"

Paul replies, "Objection, relates to the doctor's state of mind at the time of the surgery." Paul looks over to his client, "Dr. Habersham, do NOT answer that question."

Hillary retaliates, "This will let us know if the intent to hurt Jessica Stanford was premeditated, but I will move on to my next question."

Paul knows Hillary doesn't give up this easily. Hillary can't resist the temptation to ask the next question, even though she knows Paul Whittington is going to object. "Dr. Habersham, how many other patients have you performed unnecessary procedures on in the past?"

"Objection. This line of questioning is meant to harass the doctor. We need to stick to the details in the chart and nothing more."

Hillary is pleased with the outcome of the deposition. Paul
Whittington's reaction to that question confirms her
suspicions that there are other patients that have been
mutilated by the doctor. She needs to find out their names.
There is no doubt in her mind that the case is all but over.
The defense doesn't have a leg to stand on, not that she
had any doubts. She can't wait to depose Jessica's parents.

***

Paul needs to find a way to alleviate the stress from the day.
As he is thinking about what to do he hears Hillary Wells
walk up behind him. "Counselor, I hope you are ready for
trial?"

"As ready as I will ever be, I guess."

***

Hillary has tried a few cases with Paul Whittington
representing the defendants, but until today she has never
really paid much attention to him. He is actually quite a
good looking man. She has never heard any rumors around
the courthouse about him being married either. "Well, I
guess I will grab a bite to eat before heading back to the
office."

"Hold up, I was thinking about blowing off a bit of steam
after today's deposition. Why don't we go eat together? I
promise we won't talk about the case."

"I don't know."

Paul grinned at her. "Come on counselor, I won't bite…
hard, I promise."

"What the hell, but you're buying."

"Deal!"

"So what do you normally do to relax after a day like today?" asked Hillary.

"Well, what I would love to do is go to this little retreat I know of along the bayou and rent a cabin. The drive is gorgeous, nothing but a long winding road, swampland and nature. Occasionally, I may see an alligator or two, but very seldom another human being. The hunting and fishing are great. My dad used to take me quail hunting out there. I'm really not much of a hunter, but I love to fish. Not only do you have the bayou, but there is a lake out there, and the fishing is fantastic. I can go out and catch plenty to eat and never have to leave. I've never left hungry that's for sure. I usually catch enough to fill my freezer.

"Sounds divine. How often do you get away?"

"Whenever I need to recharge my batteries, or after extremely stressful cases. What do you do to relax?"

"I believe in retail therapy."

Paul chuckles at that comment. "I can't remember the last time I went shopping to just go. I hate to shop."

Now it's Hillary's turn to laugh. "It's my one indulgence in life. I love to shop. Of course, it could be due to the fact that growing up, there was never any extra money to actually go shopping."

"Are you from around here?"

"No, I grew up in a small town in Texas, but my father and I often came fishing over here. I fell in love with the area, which is why I decided to settle down here instead of back home."

"I don't see you as a fisherman, excuse me fisherwoman."

"I bet that I can out fish you any day of the week."

"I may have to take you up on that bet. What are you doing this weekend?"

Hillary feels a tingle run through her body as she thinks about spending time alone with Paul, "So counselor, are you always this expeditious?"

"No, usually I stop and think things through before acting. However, you challenged my manhood. I can't let that slip by me."

"I'm so sorry. I didn't mean to bruise your precious ego."

"Well, agree to go out with me this weekend and let me prove my fishing skill, and I will forgive you."

"I don't know. We are working on opposite sides of a case, or have you forgotten?"

"Come on counselor, it's just fishing. We did manage to get through a meal without talking about the case, and something tells me we can make it through a whole day without talking about it. I'm sure we can find plenty of interesting things to do. Besides, I really would rather not talk about my client. Would you like to bring a chaperone to make sure that I am on my best behavior?"

"That won't be necessary. Why not, I'll do it. If you have the fishing poles, I'll get the bait."

"I have the fishing poles, but I asked you to go fishing. I can get the bait."

"Nope, I plan on getting the bait. I have a special place where I get my mine. After all, I do have a bet to win."

***

The morning of the fishing trip Paul makes sure he has a blanket and the picnic basket packed. He had asked his housekeeper to make him something special, as he wasn't sure what to bring. Looking inside the basket he sees that she has put together some brie and crackers along with a bottle of chardonnay and glasses. There is also an antipasto plate and smoked turkey, havarti cheese and apricot spread on homemade croissant rolls. Hilda even packed a mouthwatering dessert assortment for them. This is nothing like what his mom packed for him when he went fishing as a kid.

Hillary's house is not at all what Paul expected. She likes to flaunt her money. The house is immense. This has to be way more house than she needs, unless she has a small army living in there.

Paul knocks on the door and waits for Hillary to answer. "Good morning. I hope you're ready to lose your bet today."

Hillary laughs. "I hope you are ready to lose. I think we need to decide on what the winner gets."

"So we are playing for a prize are we? I have a few suggestions."

"Down boy. I have an idea on what I want, and I take it you do too. Let's make this interesting then, shall we. I have a function that I want to go to next weekend, and still don't have a date for it. If I win, you have to go as my date. If I lose you get to choose where we go to next."

Paul gives her a wicked grin, "That's not nearly as fun as what I had in mind. Before I agree to this bet. What kind of function is it that you want me to attend?"

"What's wrong? Are you scared I am going to win the bet?"

"Absolutely not! Just curious is all."

"Well, since you aren't worried, then it shouldn't matter. However, to be fair I will let you know. I have a charity ball and silent auction that I plan to attend. The fundraiser is for the National Multiple Sclerosis Society. We are hoping it will be one of the biggest fundraisers of the year."

"Sounds like a good cause, but I have to be honest, I hate balls. I can think of way better things to do with my time."

"Oh come, on it will be lots of fun. I have a band arranged that will play different types of music throughout the night and there will be a variety of delicious food to choose from. Not to mention several big companies have donated quite a few nice prizes that will be auctioned off. And, to top it all off, you will get to spend the evening dancing with me."

As they drive to Paul's favorite fishing spot, they continue their talk. "So, from the way you were talking, it sounds as if you are on the committee. "

"I am. My mom has Multiple Sclerosis. I saw firsthand how the disease not only affects the patient, but the family as well. I try to help as much as I can with raising money for the MS Society. They use the money for so many things; educating people about the disease, helping patients purchase their medication, research, and so on. I have been trying to talk my mom into moving here with me since my dad passed away, but she refuses to move. She can be so stubborn at times."

"So now I know where you must get that stubborn streak of yours."

"I never thought about it, but I guess so. At least it comes honestly."

"So, what made you become an attorney?"

"I had this vision of righting all the wrongs of the world, and decided that becoming a lawyer was the best way to do it. What about you?"

"Nothing as dramatic as you. I guess you could say it is a family thing. My dad and granddad were both attorneys. It must be in my blood."

Before Paul knows it, they are at the fishing spot. The trip seemed to be faster than normal. He almost hates to be at their destination.

Hillary looks around, "I'm impressed. I was expecting you to bring me to some little secluded lake, not the river. Plus, didn't you say it was on the bayou?"

"You are sworn to secrecy about this spot. Besides, technically we will be on the bayou. We are going to have to walk a little bit if that's okay, but there is a spot up ahead where a small bayou meets the Mississippi River. The fish seem to love hanging out there. There is also a lake where the cabin is."

"I swear my lips are sealed about your secret location. My dad had a few spots like that and would never tell anyone where he would take me fishing. He was afraid once it became public knowledge, that people would take over, and he wouldn't be able to catch the same amount of fish."

Paul took all of their supplies out of the trunk and they headed to the fishing spot.

Hillary notices all the goodies he is pulling out of the trunk, "I see you must have been a boy scout when you were young."

"I just wanted to be prepared in case you got hungry or bored watching me bring in all the fish."

Hillary laughs at this comment. "Come on Counselor, it's time to put your foot where your mouth is."

"So, you never told me what your secret weapon is."

"You will see soon enough."

Once they have everything set up and are ready to bait the hooks, Hillary opened up the container. The smell nearly knocked Paul out. "What the hell is in here? I can't believe you actually put this in my car."

"Relax, I had it wrapped well, so I knew it wouldn't spill."

"Well, it sure as hell isn't going back in the trunk of my car. I will never get that smell out of there now that the container is open. You never did say what it is."

"An old trick my dad taught me. Cheap dog food soaked in pork blood."

"That's just gross."

Hillary is laughing so hard she actually has tears coming out of her eyes. "We were so poor that if we couldn't dig up enough worms, my dad would use whatever was handy. He found out by accident that the catfish would go for the dog food. The only problem is the dry dog food was too hard to put on the hook, so my dad experimented. He found that water turned the food to mush, but pig blood would congeal the dog food."

"Do I want to know how he had pig blood handy?"

"He raised and slaughtered pigs. Out of curiosity one day, he decided to see what happened. Man the fish went nuts for it. Basically, he invented his own stink bait."

"I'm impressed. I don't think I could have ever been that ingenious."

"When you are poor, you learn how to be inventive. Dad always told us money doesn't grow on trees, but if you want something bad enough you can make it happen. One way or another, without ever doing anything illegal, he made things happen."

After an hour of fishing, Paul had to admit defeat. Hillary was slaying the fish, and it was becoming pathetic how bad he was losing. "I don't know how you do it, but I can't seem to catch up. I say we call it an afternoon, let's wash up and eat."

"So, I never peeked into the basket, what all did you pack?"

"Hilda, my housekeeper, packed lots of goodies for us. There is brie, antipasto, sandwiches, dessert and even wine."

"I'm impressed, counselor. I expected you to take all the credit."

"No, I know better. Besides, if you ever taste my cooking, you will know I didn't make anything in here. Why start a relationship on lies?"

"So, is that what this is? The beginning of a relationship?"

"I'm not sure, but I would like to see where this leads if you are up to it."

"Hmm, I've never dated a defense attorney. I'm not sure what to think about dating someone from the dark side of the law."

"Oh, you are just such a comedian, aren't you?"

"I'd like to think so."

"So, what do you say about another date?"

"I definitely think there is some chemistry between us. Besides, maybe we should know a little more about each other before showing up arm in arm to the charity ball."

"So, I guess there is no getting out of that, is there?"

"Nope, and make sure you bring your checkbook."

Chapter 36

It's the night of the charity ball and Paul arrives at Hillary's house fifteen minutes early. When she opens the door, she takes his breath away. There is no doubt in his mind that she will be the most gorgeous woman there tonight. The green of her dress matches her eyes perfectly, giving an even more lustrous look to them. Her olive complexion seemed to sparkle in the moonlight.

He leans down to kiss her, making sure not mess up her makeup. "You look absolutely gorgeous. I am going to be the luckiest man there."

"Flattery just might get you everywhere tonight."

"Oh yeah. Hmm, sounds very promising."

"Easy, big boy. You have to get through the fundraiser first. Besides, it may all depend on how much money you help me raise."

She sees the limousine waiting for them, "Now I truly feel like Cinderella."

"I figured parking would be a nightmare, plus this way we don't have to worry with a designated driver if we both decide to drink."

"I like the way you think, counselor."

Once at the gala, Paul looks around at the setup and is truly impressed. The ambiance is elegant and totally fitting those attending. Everywhere he looks, he sees people dressed to impress. As if the most important thing tonight isn't how much money is raised, but which woman's dress and jewelry outshines the rest. Trophy wives hang on the arms of their husbands. Their expensive dresses of course have to be paired with the correct fancy jewels. Most of the women have diamonds and other expensive stones dripping off of them. Paul has a feeling most of these women are wearing a small fortune, possibly valued at more than his house even. He swears the diamond on one lady's hand is as big as a football.

Paul grabs two flutes of champagne and goes in search of his date. The band is playing classical music and the dance floor is packed. So far it looks as if everyone is thoroughly enjoying themselves. The food and booze seem to flow freely. There are bite size beef wellingtons that are out of this world, as are the crab cakes. There is a silent auction, where bidders write the amount they want to spend on each item and constantly try to outbid their competition. It makes the experience all the more enjoyable. Bidders are constantly watching the prices, in case someone comes and outbid their latest offer. The items include artwork, vacation packages, custom designed jewelry, and much more. Looking at the amounts items are going for, he realizes it will definitely be a profitable night for the fundraiser. Paul bids on a couple of items, but he soon realizes that these people are way out of his league. He doubts he will ever make the kind of money these people must bring in.

Paul notices Hillary is talking to another couple, and realizes as he is walking up to them that it is the Stanfords. He knew there was a chance they would meet up tonight, but he doesn't want to make Hillary feel awkward.

Hillary makes the introductions, "Mr. and Mrs. Sanford, I'm not sure if you have met Paul Whittington."

Mr. Sanford shakes his hand. "We've never been formally introduced. It's very nice to meet you sir."

"It's a pleasure to meet you, Mr. and Mrs. Sanford." They stand around and make a little idle chit chat before they part ways.

He glances over at Hillary, "That was awkward, don't you think?"

"It went better than I thought it would. I wasn't sure if they were even coming tonight. Ever since news of the lawsuit went public, some unwanted attention has been drawn their way. Some of their friends are also friends of Dr. Habersham, and they don't believe the Stanfords should have filed suit."

"I do feel for them."

"I know, and that is going to be the last I talk about the case."

"So counselor, do you have to hang around a little longer?"

"No, I don't. Why don't we head back to my house?"

"Your limo awaits, my dear."

Chapter 37

Dr. Jeffery Cole is reviewing Shane Bryant's latest MRI. Now he knows why, after months of physical therapy, Shane's range of motion in his shoulder is still showing no improvement. After Jessica's case, Dr. Cole knew he would have to get a better look at Shane's shoulder. Dr. Habersham had also operated on him. Dr. Cole had a good idea of what the MRI would show. Sure enough, a bone fragment is missing from Shane's shoulder.

"Mrs. Bryant, Shane, I am afraid I have some disturbing news for you. The latest MRI has shown why you are still experiencing pain and limited range of motion. There is a small shard of bone missing in your shoulder." Dr. Cole pulls up the MRI image and points out where the missing piece of bone should be. "Unfortunately, it is near the socket, which is what is causing the immense pain. It seems as though the nerves are possibly getting caught in the small gap."

"Was this something that the first surgeon missed?"

"Unfortunately, I'm not sure he did. There is a chance, a very slight chance, that this doctor may have done this on purpose."

"What do you mean on purpose?"

"Have you been paying attention to the news lately?"

"No, I've been busy working."

"Dr. Habersham is being sued for medical malpractice. Actually, I believe the case is getting ready to go to trial. The only reason I am bringing this up is because the plaintiff had a similar experience to your son's. Dr. Habersham removed a part of the young girl's ankle bone. I am afraid the same thing may have happened to Shane."

Dr. Cole can tell Mrs. Bryant is furious. "You would think the hospital would let his patients know."

"They are currently reviewing all of the medical records to see who needs to be contacted. Unfortunately, none of the modifications Dr. Habersham performed on his patients were documented."

"So, where does that leave us? What needs to be done for this to be corrected for Shane?"

"I wish I had some good news for you, but I don't. Shane will need to go through another operation to repair his shoulder. I will basically have to use an artificial bone to repair the damage. Since Shane is likely to have one or two more growth spurts he might have to have several more surgeries. As the bones grow, the artificial bone will have to be replaced."

"So he will have more medical expenses in the future?"

"Yes. From a professional standpoint I would suggest you get in contact with the plaintiff's attorney that is currently suing Dr. Habersham. They are already familiar with the situation and might be able to help you out. This could possibly help you with the upcoming medical bills."

"Thank you Dr. Cole. I will try to locate that name and number this afternoon."

"I have her business card, but please don't let anyone know that I referred you to her. Again, I am sorry about all of this. Dr. Habersham was a well-respected trauma surgeon. This has come as quite a shock to all of us."

"His bedside manner left a lot to be desired, but I agree, he did come highly recommended."

Dr. Cole notices through all of this Shane has not said a word.

***

Shane Bryant is fuming inside. He wants to yell at the doctor giving him this devastating news, but this doctor isn't to blame. All this happened because he was too lazy to drive to a store a few miles away. His mom had warned him about stopping at that gas station. Now he will have to endure more surgeries and possibly permanent injury to his shoulder. Where does all this leave him as he gets older?

Shane finally speaks up, anger clearly in his voice. "So, is this doctor still practicing?"

Dr. Cole answers him, "No, son, he is not. The hospital has suspended his license to practice here and the State of Louisiana has a hearing scheduled to revoke his medical license."

"What gave him the right to do this?"

"Nothing at all gave him the right. I honestly don't know what possessed him to do this to his patients."

Chapter 38

Today is the day trial begins. Morning sunlight filters in through the windows of the courtroom, causing the paneled walls to gleam. My attorney believes I am making a mistake and that we should make a last minute settlement offer. Once again, I refuse.

The bailiff gets everyone's attention, "All rise! Court is now in session. The Honorable Judge Hal Daigle presiding."

Judge Daigle is an older judge, who should have retired years ago. He looks to be a stuffy old judge, who takes crap off of no one.

"Good morning, counselors. I take it since we are all still here; there was no last minute settlement talk. Well then, let's begin with the jury selection, shall we? I want it understood that I will not put up with any grandstanding during jury selection. I want this to be a quick process, so that we can get on to the business at hand. Is that understood?"

In unison both counselors state, "Yes, your honor."

"Well, let's get the voir dire underway then." Voir dire is part of the jury selection process. It helps the attorneys determine the competency of a juror.

The judge turns to the potential jurors and addresses them, "Ladies and gentlemen, this is the case of Stanford vs. Habersham. This plaintiff is a minor and the defendant operated on her ankle. The plaintiff's parents are alleging that the doctor intentionally damaged her ankle during the surgery. The defendant denies any such negligence.

I realize for some of you, jury duty is impossible, maybe missing work for the period of this trial will cause a financial hardship or you have some sort of health problem. Whatever the reason, now is the time to let me know. Is that understood?"

The roomful of prospective jurors grows quiet, almost is if hanging on to every word the judge has to say. They have been waiting all morning to find out about the potential case they might be sitting through. The jurors state in unison, "Yes sir."

***

Paul Whittington feels as if his whole body is shaking. He would rather be any place but here today. No matter how hard he or the insurance carrier pushed, they could not get Dr. Habersham to agree to a settlement. Looking around, he wonders if anyone can tell he is trembling. He arranges his files on the desk to give the appearance that he is prepared to defend his client.

This is the first time in his career that he has felt ill before a trial. Why didn't he back out of this case? He should have insisted his partner take it.

Jury selection is going better than Paul Whittington expected. By lunch time they have their twelve men and women in the jury box.

The judge bangs his gavel, "I'm impressed counselors. I thought this would be a long drawn out process even with my warning. Let's break for lunch and return at two."

After court is back in session, the judge gives the jury some last minute instructions. After the judge is done with his instructions it's time for opening arguments.

The plaintiff's attorney is the first to speak to the jury; she stands slowly and addresses the jury box. She oozes confidence. Paul watches the jurors as she speaks. They seem to be hanging on to her every word. He notices several of the men on the panel are checking her out.

"Your Honor, ladies and gentlemen of the jury, what you are about to hear is a tragic story. A story filled with arrogance and maliciousness. The facts of this story are horrific. The life of this poor young girl and her parents will never be the same. I will show you that through the arrogance of the defendant, he has stolen the plaintiff's childhood and any future she or her parents may have dreamed of for her. Because of the malicious actions of the defendant, my client can no longer walk and will have to endure numerous painful surgeries to correct her ankle. The pain and suffering my client will have to endure is outrageous! After hearing of the defendant's actions, you will demand justice! You will be right to do so."

Paul Whittington now has to make his opening statement to the jury. He knows this is a hopeless case. There is nothing that he can say that will make what his client did right. "Your honor, ladies and gentlemen, my client is a trauma surgeon. A trauma surgeon's job is to mend broken bones and damaged tissue, and remove foreign objects. These surgeons typically work in conjunction with emergency rooms and collaborate with other specialty surgeons to transition patients from critical to stable condition. What happened to the plaintiff is a tragedy, but the care he gave to her that night was some of the best work he could have done on her ankle. However, once the patient was transferred to the orthopedic surgeon, he cannot testify as to what happened there."

Paul knows it was a long shot, pushing the possible blame off of Dr. Habersham; the evidence does not support it at all. As the plaintiff's attorney calls the expert witnesses and shows the supporting evidence, there is no denying what the doctor did. The expert witnesses' testimony rips apart his client, from stem to stern.

***

I can't help but be struck by the theatrical quality of the legal system. This is no TV drama playing out, but my medical career on the line. The tension of the moment is nerve racking. Any moment now I will wake up from this nightmare. All because the parents of one insipid young girl found out a small piece of her ankle had been removed during surgery. After this, my attorney has informed me, there will most probably be criminal charges brought against me. The District Attorney is close friends with the little girl's parents and doesn't believe a doctor should take it upon himself to alter a person's body without informed consent. Well, if I had informed the parents of what I had planned on doing, they would have denied me the research.

I look at the crowd in the courtroom and noticed several of my colleagues and nurses from the hospital. Rumor is they are glad this happened, that they thought it was time I was brought down a notch or two. Nurse Boudreaux is here. From what I have heard, she is desperately hoping they find me guilty. The hospital has reopened the case regarding her alleged malpractice during the surgery of Samuel Bellue. When the experiments that I had been conducting over the past few years came to light, the hospital realized I may have been to blame for that as well. In an attempt at kindness, I accepted full blame for that for her. No matter how vindictive I am, Nurse Boudreaux is, in all honesty, a very good nurse and the hospital needs more nurses like her.

Being forced to sit in this courtroom is humiliating though. I am a top rate surgeon; no other surgeon at the hospital can hold a candle to my skill. Now these people who can't wait to see my career come to an end are watching the case play out before them. My entire life is unraveling, my career is down the drain, and they are all thrilled to be here watching. No hospital will touch me after this, and neither will an insurance carrier.

The recent publicity has brought instant notoriety to the case. It is standing room only in the courtroom. People are forced to stand along the back wall to watch.

St. Anne's has suspended my privileges in a vicious and capricious move. Their rationale is that they feel that all the patients I have operated on will want to find out if I made any modifications to them. If there are other malpractice suits out there, I am sure they are going to come to light now. As of yet, a malpractice suit has not been filed by Jude Hudson, but I have a feeling it is coming. The Stanfords attorney is young and aggressive, and she is wondering how many more malpractice cases are out there. She has been pressuring the hospital to inform my patients of the possible malpractice cases in hopes of obtaining more clients. After all these years, this is my first malpractice lawsuit, so I guess I should be grateful. Most of my colleagues have had to suffer through this at least twice by now.

Paul Whittington urged me to settle early on. I refused. Surely the jury will see the reasoning. My attorney has ordered me to stay calm and controlled in the courtroom. He doesn't want me on the stand at all. He sees no reason to allow the plaintiff's attorney to cross-examine me. After all the heartache, anxiety and tears I have caused the little girl's family, he feels that their attorney will try to discredit me in any way, shape or form. He is also worried that I will come unglued on the stand and start spouting off about how I am a God in the OR, and the parents should be thankful I operated on their precious little girl. This is correct, of course.

The plaintiff's attorney's final argument seals the verdict. The final nail in the coffin is the plea for sympathy for her poor, hobbled, limping self-pitying client.

Paul Whittington knows there is no way he can compete with her final argument. He talks about his client's background, his education and his experience in trauma surgery, making sure he puts emphasize on the number of successful surgeries.

Now we have to await the jury's decision. The verdict should be read shortly. Maybe I shouldn't have been so arrogant in the beginning and settled out of court like the hospital. Now my arrogance may cost me more than I bargained for.

The waiting is difficult. Now it is the jury's turn to play God with my life. I must say, I don't like the shoe being on the other foot.

***

Paul Whittington steps outside of the courthouse for a brief period. He is extremely grateful that the oppressive heat of the summer is finally diminishing. It is still hot outside, but nowhere near what it has been. This summer has to be one of the worst in a long time.

The jury is sequestered in the back of the courthouse, working on their verdict. The judge will let them know shortly if they can go home for a while, or if they need to stick around the courthouse. Paul doesn't think it will take long for the jurors to make their decision. In fact, he looks for it to be over with fairly quickly now that closing arguments are over with. This has to be the worst case of his career. During the course of today's trial, he has sweated so much under his suit, that his shirt is no longer crisp and fresh. The plaintiff's attorney had him feeling like a fool. If only they could have convinced Dr. Habersham to settle early on, and not go through this mockery of a trial. His track record is shot with this one trial. Damn that stubborn doctor and his cocky attitude. Paul swears this case has given him a head full of gray hair, and the damned problem is even after this case is over, with what he knows, there will be more in its wake. Maybe with a guilty verdict, he can persuade Habersham to settle for policy limits in the future. Although, he more than likely won't have any money left after this case is over with.

Paul Whittington hears the bailiff calling everyone back into the courthouse. With his head hung low, he walks back into the courtroom.

***

I see my attorney as he enters the room. He looks defeated. I'm not sure if it's the tension from the trial, the warmth of the courtroom or the cavalier attitude of the plaintiff's attorney that is grating on my nerves.

The clerk looks at me with smugness on her face, "Will the defendant please rise."

I stand and face the jury. The jurors are staring at me with contempt in their eyes.

The clerk continues, "Foreman, has a verdict been reached?"

"Yes."

"Bailiff, please get the verdict from the Foreman."

The Bailiff delivers the sheet of paper to the judge. The judge reads the note before handing the paper to the clerk. The clerk seems to take an inordinately long time, enjoying making me wait for the verdict. It is almost as if she is taunting, mocking me. "What say you Foreman?"

"We find in the plaintiff's favor."

I look around the room. With those simple words, my life is over.   It is done. This verdict seals the verdict in the criminal case, too. I know with this verdict the district attorney will be filing criminal charges against me. On top of that, the community has had enough of me. Even without any more charges or allegations, my medical license has been suspended and is likely to be revoked. I'm not sure where to go to next. I will have to move away from here, now that I'm unable to practice medicine in the State of Louisiana. Maybe there is another state that will look the other way, but I doubt it. Before the trial, I liquidated most of my assets. Even if the family tries to sue me for the remainder of the award, there is no chance in hell they will get it from me. I still can't imagine doing anything other than surgery. The drama and excitement of the operating room is my high.

Maybe I should consider moving to another country; one where they won't check my background, and will just be grateful a surgeon wants to work there. It's not like I need the money. The first thing I plan on doing, though, is taking a long vacation. Maybe I will go to Mexico, or somewhere that does not allow extradition.